CHAPTER I

As the present century was in his tee morning he made his way to the large iror Academy for Young Girls, on Chiswick Mall, a large coach firmly, with two large horses in flamboyant harnesses, driven by a large coachman in a tricorn and wig, at the rate of four miles an hour. A black servant, who was resting on the box next to the fat coachman, unfolded his horny legs as soon as the crew stopped in front of Miss Pinkerton's shiny brass plaque, and as he tugged on the bell, in the least a score of young heads were seen narrow windows of the stately old brick house. Much more, the astute observer might have recognized the little red nose of sweet Miss Jemima Pinkerton herself, towering above a few pots of geranium in that lady's living room window.

"This is Mrs. Sedley's coach, sister," said Miss Jemima. - Sambo, the black servant, has just rung, and the coachman has a new red waistcoat.

" Do -you completed all necessary preparations from Miss Sedley, Miss Jemima ? " Askcd Miss Pinkerton herself, that majestic lady; the Semiramis of Hammersmith, the friend of Dr Johnson, the correspondent of Mrs Chapone herself.

"The girls got up at four o'clock this morning, packing her trunks, sister," replied Miss Jemima; "We made him a bow pot.

"Say a bouquet, Sister Jemima, it's more distinguished.

" Well , a notebook as big as a haystack ; I put two bottles of wallflower water for Mrs. Sedley, and the receipt for doing so, in Amelia's box. "

"And I hope, Miss Jemima, you made a copy of Miss Sedley's account. That's it, is n't it? All right - ninety-three pounds, four shillings. to address to John Sedley, squire, and to seal this note which I wrote to his lady.

In Miss Jemima's eyes an autograph letter from her sister, Miss Pinkerton, was the object of as deep reverence as a letter from a sovereign would have been . It was not until her pupils were leaving the school, or when they were about to get married, and once, when poor Miss Birch died of scarlet fever, that Miss Pinkerton wrote personally to the parents of her pupils; and it was Jemima's opinion that if anything could console Mrs. Birch for the loss of her daughter, it would be that pious and eloquent composition in which Miss Pinkerton announced the event.

In this case, Miss Pinkerton's "ticket " had the following effect :

The Mall, Chiswick, June 15-18

MADAME, - After her six years of residence at the Mall, I have the honor and the happiness to present Miss Amelia Sedley to her parents, like a young woman not unworthy of occupying a suitable place in their polite and refined circle. These virtues which characterize the young English lady, these accomplishments which become her birth and her condition, will not be lacking in the amiable Miss Sedley, whose INDUSTRY and OBEDIENCE made her loved by her instructors, and whose delicious sweetness of character charmed her and her YOUNG companions.

In music, dance, spelling, all kinds of embroidery and needlework, she will be found to have made her friends' dearest wishes come true. In geography, there is still a lot to be desired; and careful and constant use of the backboard, for four hours a day for the next three years, is recommended as necessary to acquire that worthy ride and car, so required for every young woman in FASHION.

In the principles of religion and morals, Miss Sedley will find herself worthy of an establishment which has been honored by the presence of the GREAT LEXICOGRAPHER and the patronage of the admirable Mrs. Chapone. When leaving the Mall, Miss Amelia takes with her the hearts of her companions, and the affectionate friendships of her mistress, who has the honor to register,

Madam,   Your   very   humble   servant,
BARBARA PINKERTON

PS: Miss Sharp is accompanying Miss
Sedley. In particular, it is requested that Miss
Sharp's stay in Russell Square not exceed ten
days. The distinguished family with which
she is engaged wishes to avail herself of her
services as soon as possible.

This letter completed, Miss Pinkerton proceeded to write her own
name and that of Miss Sedley on the cover page of Johnson's
Dictionary, an interesting work which she invariably presented to her
scholars when they left the Mall. On the cover was a copy
of " Lines Addressed to a Young Woman Leaving Miss Pinkerton's
School at the Mall ; by the late venerable doctor Samuel
Johnson. " Indeed, the name of the lexicographer was always on the
lips of this majestic woman, and that visit had made him was because
of his reputation and his fortune.

Having received the order from her older sister to
take "the Dictionary" out of the cupboard, Miss Jemima had extracted
two copies of the book from the receptacle in question. When Miss
Pinkerton had finished registering the first, Jemima, looking a little
dubious and timid, handed her the second.

" Who is it for, Miss Jemima?" said Miss Pinkerton with dreadful
coldness.

"For Becky Sharp," Jemima replied, very shaking and blushing
on her parched face and neck, turning her back on her sister. "For
Becky Sharp: she's going too."

"MRS JEMIMA! " Cried Miss Pinkerton, in the larger
capitals. "Are you sane? Replace the Dixonary in the closet, and never
venture to take such liberty in the future.

"Well, sister, it's only two and nine pence, and poor Becky will
be miserable if she doesn't have one."

" Send me Miss Sedley instantly, " said Miss Pinkerton. And so, venturing not to say another word, poor Jemima walked away, extremely agitated and nervous.

Miss Sedley's dad was a merchant in London, and a man of some wealth; while Miss Sharp was a student intern, for which Miss Pinkerton had done, as she thought, enough, without bestowing upon her by parting with the great honor of the Dixonary.

Although it is necessary to trust the letters of the schoolmistresses neither more nor less than the epitaphs of the cemeteries; however, as it sometimes happens that a person leaves this life which truly deserves all the praise that the stonecutter carves on their bones; who IS a good Christian, a good parent, a good child, a wife or a husband ; who truly leaves an inconsolable family to mourn their loss ; thus, in the academies of the male and female sex, it happens from time to time that the pupil is fully worthy of the praise lavished by the disinterested teacher. Now, Miss Amelia Sedley was a young woman of this singular species ; and not only deserved everything Miss Pinkerton said in her praise, but had many charming qualities that this pompous old woman Minerva could not see, because of the differences in rank and age between her pupil and herself.

Because she couldn't just sing like a lark, or a Mrs. Billington, and dance like Hillisberg or Parisot; and embroider beautifully; and comes out together with a Dixonary himself; but she had a heart so benevolent, smiling, tender, gentle and generous, that she won the love of all who approached her, from Minerva herself to the poor girl in the back kitchen and to the woman. one-eyed girl, who was allowed to sell her wares once a week to the ladies in the mall. She had twelve intimate and intimate friends out of the twenty-four young ladies. Even the envious Miss Briggs never spoke ill of her; the tall and powerful Miss Saltire (Lord Dexter's granddaughter) admitted her figure was distinguished; and as to Miss Swartz, the rich woolly haired mulatto of Saint-Kitt's, the day Amelia left she was in such a tearful passion that they were obliged to send for Dr. Floss, and the half warns of salvolatility. Miss Pinkerton's attachment was, as may be supposed from the high position and eminent virtues of this lady, calm and dignified; but Miss Jemima had already moaned several times at the idea of Amelia's departure; and, had it not been for her sister's fear, she would have become completely hysterical, like the heiress (who paid double) of Saint-Kitt's. Such luxury of grief, however, is only allowed to salon residents. Honest Jemima had all the bills, and the laundry, and the mending, and the puddings, and the plate and the dishes, and the servants to watch. But why talk about her? It is likely that we will not hear from her again from that moment at the end of time, and that when the great filigree iron gates are once closed over her, she and her ugly sister will never come out in. this little world of history.

But as we are going to see a lot of Amélie, there is no harm in saying, at the beginning of our knowledge, that she was a dear little creature; and it is a great mercy, both in life and in novels, which (and especially these latter) abound in scoundrels of the darkest sort, that we must have as a constant companion such a naive and good-natured person . As she is not a hero, there is no need to describe her person; indeed, I fear that her nose is rather short than otherwise, and her cheeks much too round and red for a heroine; but her face reddened with rosy health, and her lips the freshest of smiles, and she had a pair of eyes which shone with the liveliest and most honest good humor, except when they filled with tears, and it was a lot as often; for the fool would weep over a dead canary; or on a mouse, which the cat may have taken possession of; or at the end of a novel, even if it was so stupid; and as for him to say a mean word, were there people tough enough to do it, well, too bad for them. Even Miss Pinkerton, that austere and divine woman, stopped scolding her after the first time, and although she understood sensibility no more than she understood algebra, gave all masters and professors special orders of treat Miss Sedley with the utmost gentleness, for harsh treatment was detrimental to her.

So that when the day of departure arrived, between her two ways of laughing and crying, Miss Sedley was greatly intrigued by what to do. She was happy to come home, yet very sad to leave school. For three days, little Laura Martin , the orphan, followed her like a little dog. She was to make and receive at least fourteen gifts, making fourteen solemn promises to write each week: " Send my letters under cover to my grandfather, the Earl of Dexter, " said Miss Saltire (who, by the way, was pretty shabby). "Do not mind the postage, but write every day, you dear darling," said Miss Swartz, brash and woolly, but generous and affectionate; and little orphan Laura Martin (who was just in the round hand), took her friend's hand and said, looking up at her face wistfully, "Amelia, when I write to you I'll call you mom." All what details, I have no doubt, JONES, who reads this book in his club, will declare them excessively stupid, trivial, talkative and ultra-sentimental. Yes; I can see Jones at this minute (rather rinsed with his mutton joint and half a pint of wine), pull out his pencil and mark under the words "idiot, twaddling" etc., and adding his own remark of "EVERYTHING" to it. absolutely TRUE. " Well, he's a great man of genius, and admires the great and the heroic in life and in novels; and therefore better to take care and go elsewhere.

Well. The flowers, gifts, trunks and chests of Miss Sedley having been arranged by Mr. Sambo in the carriage, as well as a very small and weathered old cowhide trunk with Miss Sharp's card neatly nailed down upon him, which was delivered by Sambo with a smile, and packed by the coachman with a corresponding sneer - the hour of parting has come; and the grief of this moment was considerably lessened by the admirable speech which Miss Pinkerton addressed to her pupil. Not that the farewell speech had prompted Amélie to philosophize, nor that he had in any way armed her with a calm, the result of a discussion; but it was intolerably boring, pompous and boring; and having the awe of her schoolmistress greatly before her eyes, Miss Sedley did not dare, in her presence, to give in to any boil of private grief. A cake and a bottle of wine were produced in the drawing-room, as on the solemn occasions of parents' visits, and these refreshments being taken, Miss Sedley was free to leave.

" You 're going to come in and say goodbye to Miss Pinkerton, Becky !" " Said Miss Jemima to a young woman whom nobody paid attention, and that went down with his own music box.

"I suppose I must," said Miss Sharp calmly, and very much to Miss Jemima; and the latter having knocked on the door and having received permission to enter, Miss Sharp came forward with a very indifferent air, and said in French and with a perfect accent: "Mademoiselle, I have come to bid you farewell."

Miss Pinkerton did not understand French; she only led those who did: but biting her lip and raising her venerable Roman nosed head (on top of which was a large and solemn turban), she said: "Miss

Sharp, I wish you good morning." As the Hammersmith Semiramis spoke, she waved a hand, both as a farewell and to give Miss Sharp the opportunity to shake one of the fingers of the hand that had been left out for this purpose.

Miss Sharp only joined her own hands with a very cold smile and bow, and utterly refused to accept the honor offered; whereupon Semiramis threw down his turban with more indignation than ever. In fact, it was a little battle between the young lady and the old one, and the latter was saddened. " Let God bless you, my child ," she said, embracing Amelia, and scowling over the shoulder of the girl towards Miss Sharp. " Come on , Becky, " said Miss Jemima, pulling the young woman with great concern, and the living room door closed on them forever.

Then came the struggle and parting below. Words refuse to say it. All the servants were there in the hall, all the dear friends, all the young ladies, the dance master who had just arrived; and there was such a fight, and hug, and kiss, and cry, with the hysterical YOOPS of Miss Swartz, the boarder, from her room, as no feather can describe it, and as the tender heart would pass. The embrace was over; they separated, that is to say, Miss Sedley separated from her friends. Miss Sharp had modestly climbed into the car a few minutes earlier. No one cried for leaving her.

Sambo with his legs bandaged slammed the coach door on his weeping young mistress. He leaps behind the car. "Stop!" cried Miss Jemima, rushing towards the gate with a package.

"These are sandwiches, my dear," she said to Amelia. " You might be hungry, you know ; and Becky, Becky Sharp, here's a book for you that my sister - meaning me - Johnson's Dixonary, you know ; you must not leave us without it. Goodbye. To continue . , tick. God bless you !

And the nice creature withdrew into the garden, overcome with emotion.

But, voila! and just as the bus was leaving, Miss Sharp put her pale face out the window and threw the book into the garden.

It almost made Jemima pass out in terror. "Well, I never " - she said - "what a daring" - Emotion kept her from finishing either sentence. The car pulled away; the great doors were closed; the bell rang for the dance lesson. The world is before the two young ladies; and so, farewell to Chiswick Mall.

CHAPTER II

In which Miss Sharp and Miss Sedley prepare to open the campaign

When Miss Sharp had performed the heroic act mentioned in the last chapter, and saw the Dixonary, flying over the pavement of the little garden, finally fall at the feet of the astonished Miss Jemima, the face of the young woman, who had previously had Carried an air of almost livid hatred, smiled perhaps hardly more pleasantly, and she fell back into the car, peace of mind, saying, "So much the worse for the Dixonary; and, thank goodness, I have no more Chiswick. "

Miss Sedley was almost as agitated at the act of defiance as Miss Jemima had been; for, consider, it was only a minute since she left school, and the six-year-old's impressions did not come back in that span of time. No, in some people these fears and terrors of youth last forever. I know, for example, an old man of sixty-eight, who said to me one morning at breakfast, his face very agitated: "I dreamed last night that I was being whipped by Doctor Raine. Fancy had taken him fifty-five years back that evening. Doctor Raine and his rod were just as horrible to him in his heart, then, at sixty-eight, as they had been at thirteen. What if the Doctor, with a big birch, had appeared to him bodily, even at the age of sixty-eight, and had said in a dreadful voice : "Boy, take off your pants ..."? Well, well, Miss Sedley was extremely alarmed by this act of insubordination.

"How could you do that, Rebecca?" she said finally, after a pause.

" Why , do you think Miss Pinkerton is going to come out and order me back to the black hole ?" " Rebecca said, laughing.

"No but-"

"I hate the whole house," continued Miss Sharp in a fury. " I hope I never see him again. I would like it to be at the bottom of the

Thames, it is the case ; and if Miss Pinkerton was there, I wouldn't choose her, I wouldn't. I would like to see the float in the water there - there, turban and all, with her train flowing after her, and her nose like the beak of a wherry.

"Silence!" cried Miss Sedley.

" Why , will the black knave tell stories ?" " Exclaimed Miss Rebecca laughed. "He can go back and tell Miss Pinkerton that I hate her with all my soul; and I wish he would; and I also wish I had a way to prove it. For two years I have had nothing but insults and indignation from him. I was treated worse than any servant in the kitchen. I never had a friend or a kind word, except from you. I was made to look after the little girls in the lower class and speak French to the Misses, until I was fed up with my mother tongue. But that speaking French to Miss Pinkerton was a great pleasure, was n't it? She doesn't know a word of French, and was too proud to admit it. I believe that's what made him separate from me; and so thank you to heaven for the French. Long live France! Long live the Emperor! Long live Bonaparte!

"O Rebecca, Rebecca, for shame!" cried Miss Sedley; for it was the greatest blasphemy that Rebecca had yet uttered; and then, in England, to say: "Long live Bonaparte!" In other words: "Long live Lucifer!" "How can you… how dare you have such mean and vengeful thoughts?"

"Revenge may be mean, but it is natural," replied Miss Rebecca. "I am not an angel." And, to tell the truth, she certainly wasn't.

For one can notice in the course of this little conversation (which took place as the coach rolled lazily along the riverside) that although Miss Rebecca Sharp had twice had the opportunity to thank Heaven, it was, in first, for ridding her of a person she hated, and second, for allowing her to lead her enemies to a kind of perplexity or confusion; neither are very gracious grounds for religious gratitude, or as would be advanced by people of a kind and comely disposition. Miss Rebecca was therefore not at all friendly or welcoming. Everyone has misused it, said this young misanthrope, and you can be pretty sure that the people everyone abuses are very deserving of the treatment they are receiving. The world is a mirror and makes each man a reflection of his own face. Frown, and he will look at you bitterly; to laugh at her and with her, and she is a joyful and kind companion ; and thus let all the young people make their choice. Certainly, if the world has neglected Miss Sharp, she has never been known to have done a good deed for anyone; nor can we expect twenty-four young girls to be all as lovable as the heroine of this work, Miss Sedley (whom we chose for the simple reason that she was the most natural of all, except that the hell prevented us from putting Miss Swartz, or Miss Crump, or Miss Hopkins, as heroine in her place!) we could not expect everyone to be of the humble and gentle temperament of Miss Amelia Sedley; should take every opportunity to overcome Rebecca's hard-heartedness and bad temper; and, by a thousand words and benevolent offices, to overcome, for once at least, his hostility towards his fellow men.

Miss Sharp's father was an artist, and in that capacity had given drawing lessons at Miss Pinkerton's school. He was an intelligent man ; a pleasant companion; a carefree student ; with a great propensity to get into debt and a penchant for the tavern. When he was drunk he would beat his wife and daughter; and the next morning, with a headache, he mocked the world for its neglect of his genius, and abused, with great skill, and sometimes with perfect reason, the imbeciles, his brother painters. As it was with the greatest difficulty that he could maintain himself, and as he owed money for a mile around Soho, where he lived, he thought of improving his situation by marrying a young woman from the French nation, which was by profession an opera. -girl. The humble vocation of his mother, Miss Sharp, was never hinted at, but later stated that the Entrechates were a noble Gascony family and that they were very proud of their descendants. And it is curious that as she advanced in life, the ancestors of this young lady increased in rank and splendor.

Rebecca's mother had done some education somewhere, and her daughter spoke French with purity and a Parisian accent. It was at this time a rather rare accomplishment, and led to his engagement to the orthodox Miss Pinkerton. Her mother having died, her father, finding himself unlikely to recover from his third attack of delirium tremens, wrote a manly and pathetic letter to Miss Pinkerton, commending the orphan child to her protection, and so descended to the grave, after two bailiffs had argued over his corpse. Rebecca was seventeen when she arrived in Chiswick, and was linked as a student intern; his duties being to speak French, as we have seen; and his privileges of living for free and, with a few guineas a year, of collecting bits of knowledge from the teachers who attended the school.

She was small and light in person; pale, blond hair and eyes usually lowered: when they looked up they were very tall, strange and attractive; so attractive that the Reverend Mr. Crisp, newly arrived from Oxford, and pastor of the Vicar of Chiswick, the Reverend Mr. Flowerdew, fell in love with Miss Sharp; being shot down by a glance of her eyes that was drawn throughout Chiswick Church, from the school bench to the reading desk. This young man in love sometimes had tea with Miss Pinkerton, to whom he had been introduced by his mother, and in fact proposed something like marriage in an intercepted note, which the one-eyed apple was instructed to deliver. Mrs. Crisp was summoned from Buxton, and abruptly carried away her darling boy; but the very idea of such an eagle in the loft at Chiswick caused a great tremor in the breast of Miss Pinkerton, who allegedly fired Miss Sharp but was bound to her by forfeit, and who did not Never could fully believe the young woman's protests that she had never exchanged a single word with Mr. Crisp, except in front of her own eyes on the two occasions she had met him at tea.

Alongside many of the facility's tall, bouncy young girls, Rebecca Sharp looked like a child. But she had the sad precocity of poverty. More than a dun had spoken and turned away from her father's door ; more than one trader had coaxed and coaxed him into good humor, and into granting one more meal. She usually sat with her father, who was very proud of his wit, and heard the speeches of several of his wild companions, often but ill-suited for a girl to hear. But she had never been a girl, she said; she had been a woman since the age of eight. Oh, why did Miss Pinkerton leave such a dangerous bird in her cage?

The point is, the old lady believed Rebecca to be the sweetest creature in the world, so admirably, on the occasions her father brought her to Chiswick, she used Rebecca to play the part of the ingenuous; and only a year before the arrangement by which Rebecca had been admitted into her house, and when Rebecca was sixteen, Miss Pinkerton majestically, and with a little speech, presented her with a doll which was, by the way, Miss Swindle's confiscated property, discovered while surreptitiously feeding them during school hours. How the father and daughter laughed on their way home after the party (it was on the occasion of the speeches, when all the teachers were invited) and how Miss Pinkerton would have raged if she had seen the cartoon of her - even the little imitator, Rebecca, managed to get her doll out. Becky used to interact with her; it was the delight of Newman Street, Gerrard Street and the artists' quarter : and the young painters, when they came to have their gin-and-water with their lazy, dissolute, intelligent, jovial senior, used to ask regularly to Rebecca if Miss Pinkerton was at home: she was also known to them, poor soul! like Mr. Lawrence or President West. Once, Rebecca had the honor of spending a few days in Chiswick; after which she brought Jemima back and erected another doll by the name of Miss Jemmy: for although this honest creature made her and gave her enough jelly and cake for three children, and a seven shillings coin at parting, the girl's sense of ridicule was far stronger than her gratitude, and she sacrificed Miss Jemmy just as ruthlessly as her sister.

The disaster happened, and she was brought to the mall to feel at home. The rigid formality of the place choked him: prayers and meals, lessons and walks, which were organized with conventual regularity, oppressed him almost beyond all endurance; and she thought back to the freedom and begging of the old Soho studio with so much regret, that everyone, herself included, thought she was consumed by her father's grief. She had a small room in the attic, where the maids could hear her walking and sobbing at night; but it was with rage, and not with sorrow. She hadn't been very concealing, until now her loneliness had taught her to pretend. She had never mingled with the world of women: her father, disapproved of as he was, was a man of talent; her conversation was a thousand times more agreeable to her than the conversation of those of her gender that she now met. The pompous vanity of the old schoolmistress, the insane good humor of her sister, the idiotic chatter and scandal of the eldest daughters, and the icy correction of the housekeepers also annoyed him; and she was not the tender and maternal heart, this unhappy girl, if not the chatter and the conversation of the youngest children, of whom she was mainly responsible for the care, could have appeased and interested her; but she lived among them two years, and no one regretted that she left. The sweet and tender Amelia Sedley was the only person she could ever get attached to ; and who could help but get attached to Amelia?

Happiness, the superior advantages of the young women who surrounded her, gave Rebecca inexpressible pains of envy. "What tunes this girl gives herself, because she's the granddaughter of an earl," she said of one of them. "How they grind their teeth and bow to this Creole, because of her hundred thousand pounds! I am a thousand times smarter and more charming than this creature, for all her wealth. I am as well brought up as the granddaughter. of the count, for all his fine pedigree; and yet everyone is beyond me here. And yet, when I was at my father's, did not men give up their gayest balls and parties to spend the evening? with me? " She decided to break free from the prison she was in anyway, and then began to act for herself, and for the first time to make related plans for the future.

She therefore took advantage of the means of study that the place offered her; and as she was already a musician and a good linguist, she quickly followed the little study course which was deemed necessary for the ladies at that time. She was practicing her music all the time, and one day, when the girls were out, and she was staying at home, she was heard playing a piece so well that Minerva thought, wisely, that she might spare herself. the costs of a master for juniors . , and hinted to Miss Sharp that she had to educate them in music for the future.

The girl refused; and for the first time, and to the astonishment of the majestic mistress of the school. "I'm here to speak French with the kids," Rebecca said sharply, "not to teach them music, and save money for you. Give me money, and I'll teach them."

Minerva was forced to give in and, of course, didn't like her from that day on. "For thirty-five years," she said with great justice, " I have never seen the individual who dared in my own house to question my authority. I fed a viper in my womb.

"A viper, a violin stick," said Miss Sharp to the old lady, almost fainting with astonishment. "You took me because I was useful. There is no question of gratitude between us. I hate this place, and want to leave it. I will do nothing here except what I have to do."

It was in vain that the old lady asked her if she knew she was talking to Miss Pinkerton? Rebecca laughed in her face, a horrible sarcastic and demonic laugh, which almost caused fits in the schoolteacher. - Give me some money, said the young girl, and get rid of me or, if you prefer, make me a good housekeeper in a noble family, you can do it please . And in their subsequent arguments, she kept coming back to this point: " Give me a situation, we hate each other and I'm good to go." "

Worthy Miss Pinkerton, though she had a Roman nose and a turban, was as tall as a pomegranate tree, and had until then been an irresistible princess, had neither will nor strength like that of her little apprentice, and in vain fought against her, and tried to intimidate her. Attempting once to scold her in public, Rebecca found the above-mentioned plan to respond to her in French, which routed the old woman. To maintain authority in his school, he had to put aside this rebel, this monster, this snake, this brand; and hearing about this time that Sir Pitt Crawley's family needed a housekeeper, she actually recommended Miss Sharp for the situation, brand and serpent as she was. "I certainly cannot," she said, "find fault with Miss Sharp's conduct except towards myself; and I must admit that her talents and achievements are of a high order. As far as the head is concerned. , at least, it does honor to the educational system followed in my establishment.

And so the schoolmistress reconciled the recommendation to her conscience, and the contracts were canceled, and the apprentice was free. The battle described here in a few lines naturally lasted a few months. And as Miss Sedley, now in her seventeenth year, was about to drop out of school and had a friendship with Miss Sharp ("that's the only point in Amelia's behavior," Minerva said, "which was not satisfactory for her mistress ") , Miss Sharp was invited by her friend to spend a week with her at home, before taking up the duties of housekeeper in a private family.

So began the world for these two young ladies. For Amelia, it was a whole new world, fresh and shiny, with all the bloom on it. It wasn't entirely new to Rebecca - (indeed, if the truth is to be told regarding the Crisp affair, the bitter woman hinted at someone, who made an affidavit to someone else, that there was a bigger matter than what was made public regarding Mr. Crisp and Miss Sharp, and that his letter was in response to another letter). But who can tell you the real truth on the matter? In any case, if Rebecca did not start the world over, she did it again.

By the time the young girls reached the Kensington toll freeway, Amelia had not forgotten her companions, but had dried her tears, and had blushed greatly and was delighted with a young officer of the Life Guards, who l 'had watched as he passed by, and said, " A beautiful girl, egad !" " And before the car arrives at Russell Square, many conversations took place about the show, and whether or not the girls wore powder and hoops when they were presented, and if it were have this honor: at the Lord Mayor's Ball, she knew she had to go. And when at last the house had arrived, Miss Amelia Sedley jumped to the arm of Sambo, a girl as happy and as beautiful as any other in all the great city of London. He and the coachman agreed on this point, as did his father and mother, as well as all the servants in the house, as they stood, curtsying and smiling in the hall to welcome their young mistress. .

You can be sure that she has shown Rebecca all the rooms in the house, and everything in each of her drawers; and his books, and his piano, and his dresses, and all his necklaces, brooches, lace and gadgets. She insisted that Rebecca accept the white carnelian and turquoise rings, as well as a soft, stranded muslin, which was too small for her now, although it suited her friend perfectly ; and she determined in her heart to ask her mother's permission to present her white cashmere shawl to her friend. Couldn't she spare him? and had not his brother Joseph just brought him two from India?

When Rebecca saw the two beautiful cashmere shawls that Joseph Sedley had brought to her sister, she said, with perfect truth, "how delicious it must be to have a brother," and easily took pity on the girl. tender Amelia to be alone in the world, an orphan with no friends or relatives.

"Not alone," said Amelia; "You know, Rebecca, I will always be your friend, and I will love you like a sister, indeed I will."

"Ah , but to have parents, like you have, good, rich, loving parents who give you whatever you ask for; and their love, which is more precious than anything! My poor dad couldn't give me anything, and I only had two dresses in the world! And then to have a brother, a beloved brother ! Oh ! how to love it!

Amélie burst out laughing.

"What ! don't you like it? you, who say you love everyone?

" Yes , of course I do - only - "

"Just what?"

"Only Joseph doesn't seem to care much whether I like him or not. He gave me two fingers to squeeze when he arrived after ten years of absence! He is very nice and kind, but he hardly ever speaks to me ; I think he likes his pipe a lot better than his "- but here Amelia has verified itself, because why would she speak badly about her brother? " He was very nice to me when I was a child, she added. ; "I was only five years old when he left.

"Is n't he very rich?" said Rebecca. "They say all Indian moguls are extremely wealthy."

"I think he has a really big income."

"And is your sister-in-law a pretty pretty woman?"

- There! Joseph is not married, said Amélie, laughing again.

Perhaps she had already mentioned the fact to Rebecca, but this young woman did not seem to remember it; indeed, swore and protested that she expected to see a number of Amelia's nephews and nieces. She was quite disappointed that Mr. Sedley was not married; she was sure Amelia had said he was, and she loved it for little kids.

"I think you must have had enough in Chiswick," said Amelia, rather surprised at the sudden tenderness on the part of her friend; and indeed, later, Miss Sharp would never have undertaken to advance opinions the untruth of which would have been so easily detected. But we must remember that she is only nineteen, little used to the art of deception, poor innocent! and to have his own experience in his own person. The meaning of the above series of questions, as translated into the heart of this resourceful young woman, was simply this: "If Mr. Joseph Sedley is rich and single, why shouldn't I marry him?" I only have a fortnight to be sure, but there is no harm in trying. " And she determined within herself to make this laudable attempt. She redoubled her caresses to Amélie; she kissed the necklace. white carnelian putting him; and swore she would never part with, ever. When the dinner bell rang, she went down, arm around the waist of his friend, as is the habit of ladies . she was so agitated at the living room door, it was hardly the courage to enter. "Sent my heart, how it beats, my dear!" she said to her friend.

"No it's not," Amelia said. - Come in, don't be afraid. Dad won't hurt you.

CHAPTER III
Rebecca is in the presence of the enemy

A VERY fat and puffy man, in buckskin and jute boots, with several huge ties that went almost up to his nose, with a red striped waistcoat and an apple green coat with steel buttons almost as big as pieces of crown (it was a dandy's morning suit or blood of those days) was reading the newspaper by the fire when the two girls entered, and bounced off her chair, and blushed excessively, and hid her face almost in his ties at this appearance.

"It's just your sister, Joseph," said Amélie, laughing and shaking the two fingers he held out. " I came home FOR GOOD, you know ; and this is my friend, Miss Sharp, whom you have heard me speak of. "

"No , never, on my word," said his head under the tie, trembling a lot, "that is to say yes, what an abominably cold weather, mademoiselle" - and with that he began to kindle everyone's fire. his strength, although it was mid-June.

"He's very handsome," Rebecca whispered to Amelia, quite loudly.

"Do you think so?" said the latter. "I will tell him."

" Honey! Not for the worlds," said Miss Sharp, starting back as shy as a fawn. She had previously bowed like a reverent virgin to the gentleman, and her modest eyes stared at the rug with such perseverance that one wondered how she could have gotten the chance to see him.

"Thanks for the lovely shawls, brother," said Amelia of the fiery poker. "Are n't they beautiful, Rebecca?"

" O heavenly ! " Said Miss Sharp, and his eyes went directly to the carpet chandelier.

Joseph still continued to snap the poker and tongs, huffing and puffing all the time, and turning as red as his yellow face allowed him to be. "I can't give you such beautiful gifts, Joseph," his sister continued, "but while I was at school, I embroidered a very nice pair of suspenders for you.

"Good God! Amelia , " cried the brother, in serious alarm," what do you mean? and, plunging with all his strength to the cord of the bell, this piece of furniture slipped from his hand, and increased the confusion of the honest fellow. "For heaven's sake, see if my buggy is at the door. I can't wait. I have to go. D—- that groom of mine. I have to go."

At that moment the father of the family entered, snapping his seals like a true British merchant. "What's the matter , Emmy?" he said.

"Joseph wants me to see if his… his stroller is at the door." What is a stroller, dad?

"It's a palanquin with one horse," said the old gentleman, who was a joker in his own way.

Joseph then burst out laughing; in which, meeting Miss Sharp's eye, he suddenly stopped, as if he had been shot.

" Is this young woman your friend?" Miss Sharp, I am very happy to see you. Have you and Emmy ever had a fight with Joseph that he wants to go?

- I promised Bonamy of our service, sir, said Joseph, to dine with him.

- O fie! didn't you tell your mother you would dine here?

"But in this dress, it's impossible."

" Look at him , isn't he handsome enough to have dinner anywhere, Miss Sharp ?" "

Whereupon, of course, Miss Sharp looked at her friend, and they both burst into laughter, very agreeable to the old man.

"Have you ever seen a pair of buckskins like Miss Pinkerton's?" he continued, pursuing his advantage.

" Merciful heavens ! Father," cried Joseph.

" There , now, I hurt his feelings. Mrs. Sedley, my dear, I hurt your son's feelings. I alluded to his buckskins. Ask Miss Sharp if I do not have it done ? Come on, Joseph, be friends with Miss Sharp, and let's all go to dinner. "

"There's a pillau, Joseph, as you like it, and daddy brought home the best turbot in Billingsgate."

"Come on , come on, sir, go down the stairs with Miss Sharp, and I'll follow with these two young women," said the father, and he took his wife and daughter's arms and walked away happily.

If Miss Rebecca Sharp had decided in her heart to make the conquest of this great beau, I don't think, ladies, that we have the right to blame her; for although the task of driving husbands away is generally, and with proper modesty, entrusted by young men to their mothers, remember that Miss Sharp had no kind relatives to arrange these delicate matters for her, and that if she had no husband for herself, there was no one else in the wide world who would take the pain away from her. What makes young people "come out " if not the noble ambition of marriage? What makes them flock to the water points ? What makes them dance until five in the morning for a whole deadly season ? What prompts them to work on piano sonatas, to learn four songs from a fashionable master in a lesson in Guinea, and to play the harp if they have nice arms and stems? neat elbows, and wearing Lincoln green toxophilite hats and feathers, but can that knock down a " desirable " young man with their murderous bows and arrows ? What prompts respectable parents to take their rugs, turn their homes upside down, and spend a fifth of their annual income on ballroom dinners and iced champagne ? Is it a pure love of their kind and a pure desire to see young people happy and dancing? Pcha ! they want to marry their daughters; and, as the honest Mrs Sedley has, in the bottom of her good heart, already arranged about twenty small plans for the settlement of her Amelia, so our beloved but unprotected Rebecca was determined to do her best to secure the husband, who was even more necessary to her than to her friend. She had a vivid imagination; moreover, she had read the Thousand and One Nights and the Geography of Guthrie; and it is a fact that while she was dressing for dinner, and after asking Amélie if her brother was very rich, she had built herself a most magnificent castle in the air, of which she was the mistress , with a husband somewhere in the background (she hadn't seen him yet, so his figure wouldn't be very clear); she had adorned herself with an infinity of shawls, turbans and diamond necklaces, and had mounted an elephant to the sound of Bluebeard's march, to pay a ceremonial visit to the Grand Mogul. Charming visions of Alnaschar! it is the happy privilege of youth to build you up, and many fanciful young creatures besides Rebecca Sharp have indulged in these delicious reveries earlier now!

Joseph Sedley was twelve years older than his sister Amelia. He was in the civil service of the East India Company, and his name appeared, at the time of this writing, in the Bengal division of the East India Register, as a collector of Boggley Wollah, an honorable and lucrative post. , as everyone knows: in In order to know to what senior positions Joseph rose in the service, the reader is referred to the same periodical.

Boggley Wollah is located in a beautiful secluded, swampy and jungly area famous for snipe shooting, and where it is not uncommon for you to be able to hunt a tiger. Ramgunge, where there is a magistrate, is only forty miles away, and there is a cavalry station thirty miles away; Joseph therefore wrote to his parents when he took possession of his collection. He had lived about eight years of his life, all by himself, in this lovely place, hardly seeing a Christian face until twice a year, when the detachment arrived to take the income he had collected, to Calcutta.

Fortunately, at this time he contracted a disease of the liver, for which he returned to Europe, and which was for him the source of great comfort and great amusement in his native country. He did not live with his family in London, but had a home of his own, as a young single gay. Before going to India he was too young to taste the delicious pleasures of a city man, and on his return he immersed himself with considerable diligence. He led his horses in the park; he dined in fashionable cabarets (for the Oriental Club was not yet invented); he frequented theaters, as was the fashion then, or appeared at the opera, laboriously dressed in tights and a cocked hat.

Back in India, and forever, he spoke of the pleasure of this period of his life with great enthusiasm, and made you understand that he and Brummel were the main cocks of the day. But he was as lonely here as he was in his jungle at Boggley Wollah. He barely knew a single soul in the metropolis: and without his doctor, and the company of his blue pill, and his liver disease, he would have had to die of loneliness. He was lazy, brooding, and good-natured ; the appearance of a lady frightened him beyond measure; that is why he rarely joined the paternal circle of Russell Square, where gaiety reigned and where his good old father's jokes frightened his self-esteem. Its mass caused Joseph much anxiety and anxiety; every now and then he desperately tried to shake off his excess fat; but his laziness and his love of good life soon won out over these attempts at reform, and he found himself at his three meals a day. He was never well dressed; but he took the greatest care to adorn his grown-up person, and spent many hours a day in this occupation. His valet made a fortune with his wardrobe: his toilet was covered with as many ointments and essences as had ever been used by an old beauty: he had tried, to give himself a size, all the straps, reinforcements and belts. then invented. Like most fat men, he made his clothes too tight and made sure they were the brightest colors and the youngest fit. When he was dressed for a long time, in the afternoon, he would go out for a walk without anyone in the park; then came back to get dressed and went to dinner without anyone in the cafe in the Piazza. He was conceited as a girl; and perhaps his extreme shyness was one of the results of his extreme vanity. If Miss Rebecca manages to get the upper hand on him, and on her first entry into life, she is a young person of extraordinary intelligence.

The first movement showed considerable skill. When she called Sedley a very handsome man, she knew that Amelia would tell her mother, who would probably tell Joseph, or who, in any case, would be delighted with the compliment paid to her son. All mothers are. If you had told Sycorax that her son Caliban was as beautiful as Apollo, she would have been delighted, witch like she was. Perhaps, too, Joseph Sedley would hear the compliment - Rebecca spoke loudly enough - and he heard, and (thinking in his heart that he was a very good man) the praise vibrated every fiber of his great. body and made it tingle. with pleasure. Then, however, came a setback. "Is the girl laughing at me?" he thought, and immediately he jumped up to the bell, and was to back down, as we have seen, when his father's jokes and his mother's pleas made him stop and stay where he was. . He led the young lady to dinner in an uncertain and restless state of mind. "Does she really think I'm handsome?" he thought, "or is she laughing at me?" We have spoken of Joseph Sedley as conceited as a girl. May heaven help us ! the girls have only to turn the tide and say to one of their sex: "She is vain as a man", and they will have a perfect reason. Bearded people are just as eager for praise, just as meticulous of their dress, just as proud of their personal advantages, just as aware of their power of fascination, as any coquette in the world.

So they went downstairs, Joseph very red and blushing, Rebecca very modest, and her green eyes lowered. She was dressed in white, with bare shoulders as white as snow - the image of youth, unprotected innocence, and virgin humble simplicity. I must be very calm, Rebecca thought, and very interested in India.

Now we heard how Mrs. Sedley made a nice curry for her son just the way he liked it, and over dinner a portion of this dish was offered to Rebecca. "What is that?" she said, turning an attractive gaze to Mr. Joseph.

" Capital ", he said. Her mouth was full of it: her face all red from the delicious gobbling exercise. "Mother, this is as good as my own curries in India."

"Oh, I have to try some, if it's an Indian dish," Miss Rebecca said. "I'm sure everything has to be good that comes from there."

" Give Miss Sharp some curry, my dear, " Mr. Sedley said with a laugh.

Rebecca had never tasted the dish before.

" Do you find it as good as all the rest of India ?" " Said Sedley.

"Oh, excellent!" Said Rebecca, who suffered torture with cayenne pepper.

"Try a chili with it, Miss Sharp," said Joseph, genuinely interested.

"A chili," Rebecca said, panting. "Oh yes!" She thought a chili was something cool, as the name mattered, and was served with it. "How fresh and green they look," she said, and put one in her mouth. It was hotter than the curry; flesh and blood could no longer take it. She put down her fork. " Water, for heaven's sake, water! She cried. Mr. Sedley burst out laughing (he was a rude man from the Stock Exchange, where people like all kinds of pranks). "They are real Indians, I assure you," he said. "Sambo, give Miss Sharp some water."

The fatherly laughter was echoed by Joseph, who found the joke capital. The ladies only smiled a little. They thought poor Rebecca was in too much pain. She would have liked to stifle old Sedley, but she swallowed her mortification as well as she had before her the abominable curry, and as soon as she could speak, she said comically and in good humor: "I should have. must have remembered the pepper that the Princess of Persia puts in the Arabian Nights cream pies. Do you put cayenne pepper in your cream pies in India, sir?

Old Sedley laughed and thought Rebecca was a good-natured girl. Joseph simply said, " Cream pies, miss ?" Our cream is very bad in Bengal. We generally use goat 's milk ; and, " God, you know, I must prefer him ! "

"You won't love ALL of India now, Miss Sharp," said the old gentleman; but when the ladies had retired after dinner, the crafty old man said to his son, "Take care, Joe, that girl is putting her cap on you."

" Pooh ! This is absurd ! " Joe said, very flattered. " I remember, sir, that there was a daughter in Dumdum, a daughter of the artillery cutler, and later married to Lance, the surgeon, who killed me in AD 4, to me and to Mulligatawney, which I told you about before dinner - a heck of a mulligatawney man - he's a magistrate at Budgebudge, and he's sure to be on the council in five years. Well, sir, the artillery has given a ball, and Quintin of the King's 14th said to me , 'Sedley,' he said, 'I'll bet you thirteen to ten that Sophy Cutler will hook you or

Mulligatawney before the rains. " Done, " I say ; and egad, sir, this bordeaux is very good. Adamson or Carbonell ? "

A slight snore was the only response: the honest stockbroker was asleep, and so the rest of Joseph's story was lost for that day. But he was always extremely communicative at a men's party, and told this delicious story time and time again to his apothecary, Dr. Gollop, when he came to inquire about the liver and the blue pill.

Disabled, Joseph Sedley settled for a bottle of Bordeaux in addition to his Madeira at dinner, and he managed to manage a few plates full of strawberries and cream, and twenty-four rout cupcakes that lay neglected in a plate near him, and certainly (for novelists have the privilege of knowing everything) he thought a lot about the girl from above. A kind, cheerful and happy young creature, he thought to himself. "How she looked at me when I picked up her handkerchief at dinner!" She dropped it twice. Who is singing in the living room?

But her modesty rushed at him with uncontrollable force. His father was asleep: his hat was in the hall: there was a cab in Southampton Row. 'I'll go see the forty thieves,' he said, 'and Miss Decamp's dance ; and he slipped gently on the pointed toes of his boots, and disappeared, without awakening his worthy relative.

- There is Joseph, said Amélie, who was looking through the open windows of the living room, while Rebecca sang on the piano.

"Miss Sharp scared him," Ms. Sedley said. "Poor Joe, why will he be so shy? "

CHAPTER IV

Green silk purse

Poor Joe's panic lasted two or three days; during which he did not visit the house, and during that time Miss Rebecca never mentioned her name. She was very respectful of Mrs. Sedley; delighted beyond measure at the bazaars; and in a whirlwind of wonder at the theater, where the good-humored lady took her. One day, Amélie had a headache and could not go to some fun party to which the two young people were invited: nothing could induce her friend to go without her. "What ! you who showed the poor orphan what happiness and love are for the first time in her life, leave you? Never ! and the green eyes looked up to heaven and filled with tears; and Mrs. Sedley could not but recognize that her daughter's friend had a charming and kind heart.

As for Mr. Sedley's jokes, Rebecca laughed at them with a cordiality and perseverance which pleased and softened this good-humored gentleman a little. Neither was it with the heads of families alone that Miss Sharp found favor. She interested Mrs. Blenkinsop by showing the deepest sympathy for the raspberry jam, which was then taking place in the housekeeper's room; she persisted in calling Sambo "Sir" and "Mr. Sambo", much to this servant's delight; and she apologized to the maid for having given her trouble ringing the bell with such gentleness and humility, that the servants' room was almost as charmed by it as the drawing room.

Once, going through some drawings Amelia had sent from school, Rebecca suddenly came across one that made her burst into tears and leave the room. It was the day Joe Sedley made his second appearance.

Amelia ran after her friend to find out the cause of this manifestation of emotion, and the good girl returned without her companion, quite affected too. "You know, her father was our drawing master, Mamma, in Chiswick, and used to do all the best parts of our drawings."

"My love! I'm sure I've always heard Miss Pinkerton say he didn't touch them, he just rode them. "It was called going up, mum. Rebecca remembers the drawing, and her dad working on it, and the idea came to her quite suddenly - and so, you know, she ..."

"The poor kid is all heart," Ms. Sedley said.

"I wish she could stay with us another week," Amelia said.

"She is evil like Miss Cutler I used to meet in Dumdum, but more beautiful. She is now married to Lance, the artillery surgeon. 14th , bet me ... "

"O Joseph, we know this story," said Amélie, laughing. "You don't mind saying that; but persuade Mum to write Sir Something

Crawley on leave for poor dear Rebecca: here she is, her eyes red with tears."

"I'm better now," the young girl said, with the sweetest smile possible, taking Mrs. Sedley's outstretched hand and kissing her respectfully. "How nice you are to me!" All of them, she added, laughing, except you, Mr. Joseph.

"Me!" said Joseph, meditating an immediate departure. " Graceful heavens ! God damn it ! Miss Sharp ! "

" Yes ; how could you be cruel enough to make me eat that horrible dish of pepper for dinner the first day I saw you? You are not as good to me as my dear Amelia . "

"He doesn't know you that well," Amelia cried.

"I challenge anyone not to be good to you, my dear," her mother said.

"The curry was essential; indeed he was, "said Joe, quite gravely. "Maybe there was NOT enough lemon juice in it, no there was NOT."

"What about the peppers?

"By Jupiter, how they made you scream! " Joe said, taken by the ridiculousness of the circumstance, and bursting into a burst of laughter that ended suddenly, as usual.

"I'll be careful how I let YOU choose for me another time," Rebecca said, as they walked downstairs for dinner. "I didn't think men liked to hurt poor, harmless girls."

"By Gad, Miss Rebecca, I wouldn't hurt you for the world."

" No, " she said, " I KNOW you wouldn't " ; then she gave it a very gentle pressure with her little hand, and withdrew it very frightened, and looked first for a moment at her face, then at the carpet rails; and I am not prepared to say that Joe's heart did not pound at this involuntary, shy and gentle little gesture of consideration on the part of the simple girl.

It was a breakthrough, and as such, perhaps, some ladies of undoubted correctness and kindness will condemn the action as immodest; but, you see, poor dear Rebecca had all this work to do for herself. If someone is too poor to have a servant, however elegant he may be, he must sweep his room: if a dear daughter does not have a dear mother to settle affairs with the young man, she must. do for itself. And oh, what a mercy that these women do not exercise their powers more often ! We cannot resist them, if they do. Let them show so little inclination, and the men immediately kneel down: old or ugly, it's all the same. And this I have posed as a positive truth. A woman with fair opportunities, and without an absolute bump, can marry WHO SHE LOVES. Only let us be thankful that the darlings are like the beasts of the field and do not know their own power. They would overcome us entirely if they did.

" Egad ! " Joseph thought upon entering the dining room, I start to feel exactly like Dumdum with Miss Cutler. Many sweet little calls, half tender, half pleasant, made her Miss Sharp about the dishes at dinner; for at that moment she was on the foot of a considerable familiarity with the family, and as for the girls, they loved each other like sisters. The unmarried girls always do, if they are in a house together for ten days.

As if she's determined to move Rebecca's plans forward in any way - what should Amelia do, but remind her brother of a promise made last Easter break - "When I was a girl in school," says - she laughed - a promise that he, Joseph, would take her to Vauxhall. "Now," she said, "that Rebecca is with us, that will be the very moment."

" O delicious ! " Said Rebecca going clap their hands; but she pulled herself together and stopped, like a modest creature as she was.

"Tonight is not night," Joe said.

"Well, tomorrow."

"Tomorrow your daddy and I are having dinner out," said Mrs. Sedley.

"Do n't you think I'm going, Mrs. Sed?" said her husband, and that a woman your age and your size must catch a cold, in such a dreadful and damp place?

"The kids have to have someone with them," cried Ms. Sedley.

" Let Joe go, " his dad laughed. "He's quite tall. At which speech even Mr. Sambo at the buffet burst out laughing, and poor fat Joe felt inclined to almost become a parricide.

"Cancel your stays!" continued the ruthless old gentleman. "Throw water in his face, Miss Sharp, or carry him upstairs: the dear creature is passed out." Poor victim! wear it; it is as light as a feather!

"If I take it, sir, I'm d ———!" roared Joseph.

"Order Mr. Jos' elephant, Sambo!" cried the father. "Send to Exeter 'Change, Sambo " ; but seeing Jos ready to cry almost in spite, the old prankster stopped laughing and said, holding out his hand to his son: me and Mr. Jos a glass of champagne. Boney himself doesn't have one in his basement, boy!

A glass of champagne gave Joseph equanimity, and before emptying the bottle, two-thirds of which he had taken as an invalid, he had agreed to take the young ladies to Vauxhall.

" Girls must each have a gentleman," said the old gentleman. "Jos will be sure to leave Emmy in the crowd, he'll be so busy with Miss Sharp here. Send him to 96 and ask George Osborne if he's coming."

At that, I have no idea why, Mrs. Sedley looked at her husband and burst out laughing. Mr. Sedley's eyes twinkled indescribably mischievously, and he looked at Amelia; and Amelia, lowering her head, blushed as only seventeen-year-old girls know how to blush, and as Miss Rebecca Sharp has never blushed in her life - at least not since she was eight, and when she was was caught stealing jam from a cupboard of her godmother. "Amelia better write a note," said her father; "And let George Osborne see what beautiful handwriting we brought back from Miss Pinkerton." Do you remember when you wrote her to come on Twelfth night, Emmy, and spelled twelfth without the f?

"That was years ago," Amelia said.

"Looks like yesterday, doesn't it, John?" said Mrs. Sedley to her husband; and that night in a conversation which took place in a front room on the second floor, in a sort of tent, hung with chintz of a rich and fantastic pattern from India, and lined with calico of a soft pink ; inside of which a sort of capital was a feather bed, on which were two pillows, on which were two round red faces, one in a laced nightcap, and the other in a simple cotton, ending by a pompom - in a READING CURTAIN, I say, Mrs. Sedley blamed her husband for his cruel behavior towards poor Joe.

"It was rather mean of you, Mr. Sedley," she said, "to torment the poor boy like that.

'My dear,' said the cotton acorn in defense of his conduct, 'Jos is far more conceited than you have ever been in your life, and that is saying a lot. and eighty ... what was that? ... maybe you had the right to be conceited ... I'm not saying no. But I have no patience with Jos and his stupid modesty. It's off Joseph, my dear, and all while the boy thinks only of himself, and what a good boy he is. I doubt, Madam, that we still have problems with him. Here is Emmy's girlfriend making love to her as hard as she can ; it is quite clear ; and if she doesn't catch it, another will. This man is meant to be the prey of the woman, as I have to continue " Change every day." It's a mercy he didn't show us for a black girl. law , my dear. But, notice my words, the first woman to fish it hooks it up.

"She 'll be leaving tomorrow, the nifty little creature," said Mrs. Sedley, with great energy.

"Why not her as good as any other, Mrs. Sedley? The girl has a white face anyway. I don't care who is marrying her. Let Joe have some fun."

And soon the voices of the two loudspeakers died down, or were replaced by the soft but not romantic music of the nose; and except when the church bells struck the hour and the keeper called him, all was quiet at John Sedley's house, Esquire, Russell Square, and the Stock Exchange.

When morning came, good-humored Mrs. Sedley no longer thought of carrying out her threats against Miss Sharp; for although nothing was more vivid, nor more common, nor more justifiable than maternal jealousy, she could not, however, bring herself to suppose that the humble, grateful and gentle little housekeeper would dare to admire such a magnificent figure as the collector. by Boggley Wollah. The petition, too, for an extension of the young woman's leave had already been dispatched, and it would be difficult to find a pretext for abruptly dismissing her.

And as if everything conspired in favor of sweet Rebecca, the very elements (although she was not inclined at first to recognize their action in her favor) intervened to help her. For on the evening appointed for the Vauxhall feast, George Osborne having come to dine and the elders of the house having gone, by invitation, to dine with Alderman Balls at Highbury Barn, there was such a thunderstorm as it only happens on Vauxhall nights, and as if forced young people, necessarily, to stay at home. Mr. Osborne didn't seem in the least bit disappointed with this event. He and Joseph Sedley drank a fair amount of Port wine one-on-one in the dining room, during which Sedley recounted a number of her best Indian stories; for he was extremely talkative in human society ; and then Miss Amelia Sedley did the honors of the salon; and these four young people spent such a comfortable evening together, that they declared that they were rather pleased with the storm than otherwise, which had caused them to delay their visit to Vauxhall.

Osborne was Sedley's godson, and had been one of the family throughout these twenty-three years. At six weeks old he had received a gift of a silver cup from John Sedley ; at six months, a coral with a whistle and golden bells; from his youth he was regularly "tipped" by the old gentleman at Christmas: and on returning to school, he remembered vividly being beaten by Joseph Sedley, when the latter was a great hobbadyhoy swagger, and George a impudent ten-year-old kid. In short, George was as familiar with the family as such daily acts of kindness and sex could make him.

" Do you remember, Sedley, how furious you were, when I cut the tassels off your burlap boots, and how Miss — hem! —How Amelia saved me from a beating, in falling to his knees and shouting at his brother Jos, not to beat little George? "

Jos remembered this remarkable circumstance perfectly, but swore he had completely forgotten it.

" Well , do you remember going down to a concert at Dr Swishtail's to see me, before going to India, and giving me half a guinea and a pat on the head ?" I always had the idea that you were at least seven feet tall. high , and I was quite astonished when you came back from India to find you no taller than me.

"How nice of Mr. Sedley to go to your school and give you the money!" cried Rebecca with accents of extreme delight.

"Yes, and after I cut the tassels off her boots too. The boys never forget this advice at school, nor the donors."

" I love jute boots ," said Rebecca. Jos Sedley, who prodigiously admired his own legs, and always wore this ornamental shoe, was extremely happy at the remark, although he pulled his legs under his chair as it was done.

" Miss Sharp ! " . Said George Osborne," that you are an artist so smart, you have to make a big historical picture of the scene boots Sedley will be represented in the skins of deer, and holding one of the boots wounded in a hand by "Another one, he must take my shirt collar. Amélie will be kneeling beside him, her little hands raised, and the painting will have a large allegorical title, like the frontispieces of the Medulla and the spelling book.

"I won't have time to do it here," Rebecca said. "I'll do it when - when I'm gone." And she lowered her voice and looked so sad and pitiful, that everyone felt how cruel her fate was and how sorry they would be to part with her.

"Oh that you can stay longer, dear Rebecca," Amelia said.

"Why?" replied the other, more sadly still. "That I could only be more miserable, not wanting to lose you?" And she turned her head away. Amélie was beginning to give in to this natural infirmity of tears which, as we have said, was one of the faults of this little animal. George Osborne looked at the two young women with moved curiosity ; and Joseph Sedley heaved something like a sigh from his big chest, as he looked down at his favorite jute boots.

"Let's go listen to some music, Miss Sedley ... Amelia," said George, who at that moment felt an extraordinary, almost irresistible urge to grab the aforementioned young woman in his arms and kiss her in front of the company; and she looked at him for a moment, and if I said that they fell in love with each other at this exact moment, I would say maybe an untruth, because the point is that these two young people had been brought up by their parents for this very purpose, and their banns had, so to speak, been read in their respective families at any time during those ten years. They went to the piano, which was situated, as pianos usually are, in the back room ; and since it was rather dark, Miss Amelia, in the simplest way in the world, put her hand in Mr. Osborne's, who, of course, could see the path between the chairs and the ottomans much better than she did. But this arrangement left Mr. Joseph Sedley alone with Rebecca at the living room table, where she was busy knitting a green silk purse.

"There is no need to ask for family secrets," Miss Sharp said. "These two said theirs.

"As soon as he has his company," said Joseph, "I believe the matter is settled. George Osborne is a man of capital.

"And your sister, the most expensive creature in the world," said Rebecca. "Happy the man who wins it! " With that, Miss Sharp sighed heavily.

When two unmarried people get together and discuss such sensitive topics as the present, a great deal of trust and intimacy is established between them. There is no need to give a special report of the conversation which now took place between Mr. Sedley and the young lady; for the conversation, as one can judge from the above specimen, was not especially spiritual or eloquent; it's rarely in private companies, or anywhere, except in very high-flying and ingenious novels . As there was music in the next room, the conversation continued, of course, in a low and becoming tone, although, moreover, the couple in the next apartment would not have been disturbed if the conversation had been so. noisy , they were so busy with their own activities.

Almost for the first time in his life, Mr. Sedley found himself talking, without the slightest shyness or hesitation, to a person of the opposite sex. Miss Rebecca asked him a lot of questions about India, which gave him the opportunity to tell many interesting anecdotes about this country and himself. He described the balls at Government House, and how they kept cool in hot weather, with punkahs, tatties, and other devices ; and he was very witty about the number of Scots that Lord Minto, the Governor General, sponsored; then he described a tiger hunt; and the way his elephant's mahout had been snatched from his seat by one of the angry animals. How thrilled Miss Rebecca was at government balls, and how she mocked the stories of the

Scottish aides-de-camp, and called Mr. Sedley a sad wicked satirical creature ; and how she was afraid of the elephant story! "For your mother's sake, dear Mr. Sedley," she said, "for the sake of all your friends, promise NEVER to go on any of these horrible expeditions.

" Pooh , pooh, Miss Sharp, " he said, pulling up his shirt collars ; "danger only makes sport more enjoyable." He had only ever been to a tiger hunt once, when the accident in question had occurred, and when he had been half-killed, not by the tiger, but by fear. And as he spoke he got pretty daring, and actually had the nerve to ask Miss Rebecca who she was knitting the green silk handbag for ? He was quite surprised and delighted with her familiar and graceful manners.

"For anyone who wants a scholarship," replied Miss Rebecca, looking at him in the sweetest winning way. Sedley was going to give one of the most eloquent speeches possible, and had started - "O Miss Sharp, how-" when a song that was played in the other room ended, and made her hear her own voice though. distinctly he stopped, blushed, and blew his nose with great agitation.

"Have you ever heard anything like your brother's eloquence?" whispered Mr. Osborne to Amelia. "Why, your friend did miracles."

"The more the better," said Miss Amelia; who, like almost all women who are worth a pin, was a matchmaker in her heart, and would have been delighted if Joseph brought a woman back to India. She had also, during these few days of constant relations, warmed to a most tender friendship for Rebecca, and had discovered in her a million virtues and lovable qualities that she had not perceived when they were together in Chiswick. For the affection of young ladies grows as fast as Jack's bean, and reaches the sky overnight. It is not a blame for them that after the marriage, this Sehnsucht nach der Liebe calms down. This is what sentimentalists, who speak in really big words, call a longing after the Ideal, and simply means that women are generally not satisfied until they have husbands and children on whom they can focus ailments, which are spent elsewhere, so to speak, in small change.

Having exhausted her small stock of songs, or having stayed long enough in the back room, it now seemed appropriate for Miss Amelia to ask her friend to sing. "You wouldn't have listened to me ," she told Mr. Osborne (although she knew she was telling a lie), "if you had heard Rebecca first."

"I give Miss Sharp a warning, however," said Osborne, "that, rightly or wrongly, I consider Miss Amelia Sedley to be the world's premier singer."

"You will hear," said Amelia; and Joseph Sedley was actually polite enough to carry the candles to the piano. Osborne has hinted that he might as well like to sit in the dark; but Miss Sedley, laughing, refused to keep him company further, and the two accordingly followed Mr. Joseph. Rebecca sang much better than her friend (although of course Osborne was free to keep his opinion), and practiced to the max, and, in fact, to the amazement of Amelia, who had never seen her so well. to play. She sang a French song which Joseph did not understand at all and which George confessed not to understand, and then a number of those simple ballads which were in fashion forty years ago, and in which the British tars, our king , poor Susan, blue-eyed Mary, etc., were the main themes. They are not, it is said, very brilliant from a musical point of view, but contain innumerable simple and good appeals to the affections, which people understood better than the lagrime, sospiri and felicita with milk and water. the eternal Donizettian music of which we are today favored.

Between the songs, a sentimental conversation began, worthy of the subject, which Sambo, after bringing the tea, the delighted cook and even Mrs. Blenkinsop, the housekeeper, deigned to listen to on the landing stage.

Among these songs, there was one, the last of the concert, and to the following effect :

Ah ! dreary and barren was the moor, Ah! The storm was strong and piercing, The roof of the cottage was well sheltered, The hearth of the cottage was bright and warm - An orphan boy in the lattice passed, And, as he marked his mirthful glow, Felt the double breath midnight, And doubly cold the fallen snow.

They marked him as he moved forward, Heart failing and limb tired; Kind voices invited him to turn and rest, And gentle faces greeted him. Dawn rises, the guest leaves , The cottage fireplace is still blazing ; May Heaven have mercy on all the poor lonely wanderers! Hear the wind on the hill!

It was the feeling of the words mentioned above, "When I'm gone," again. As she came to the last words, "Miss Sharp's deep voice faltered." Everyone felt the allusion to her departure and her unhappy orphan state. Music-loving and tender-hearted Joseph Sedley was in a state of rapture as the song performed, and deeply touched at its conclusion. If he had had the courage; if George and Miss Sedley had remained, as the former suggested, in the back room, Joseph Sedley's celibacy would have been terminated, and this work would never have been written. But at the end of the song, Rebecca left the piano, and, giving her hand to Amelia, went into the twilight of the front room ; and, at this point, Mr. Sambo made his appearance with a tray, containing sandwiches, jellies, and a few glittering glasses and decanters, upon which Joseph Sedley's attention was immediately fixed. When the parents of the Sedley house returned from their dinner, they found the young men so busy talking that they did not hear the car coming, and Mr. Joseph was saying, "My dear Miss Sharp, a teaspoon of jelly to recruit you after your immense - your - your delicious efforts. "

" Well done Jos ! " Said Sedley; Hearing the jokes in that well-known voice, Jos instantly fell back into alarmed silence, and quickly left. He didn't stay awake all night wondering whether or not he was in love with Miss Sharp; the passion of love never interfered with the appetite or the sleep of Mr. Joseph Sedley; but he thought how delicious it would be to hear songs like those after Cutcherry - what a distinguished girl she was - how she could speak French better than the Lady of the Governor General herself - and what a sensation she would make in Calcutta. balls. It is obvious that the poor devil is in love with me, he thought. "She's as rich as most of the girls who come to India. I could go further, and do worse, egad!" And in these meditations he fell asleep.

How Miss Sharp stayed awake, thinking, will he come or not tomorrow? does not need to be said here. Tomorrow came, and, sure as fate, Mr. Joseph Sedley made his appearance before lunch. He had never been known before to bestow such honor on Russell Square. George Osborne was already there somehow (sadly " turning off " Amelia, who wrote to her twelve dearest friends at Chiswick Mall), and Rebecca was busy with her work yesterday. As Joe's buggy arrived, and as, after its usual thunder and pompous bustle at the door, the former Boggley Wollah collector climbed the stairs to the living room, warned glances were telegraphed between Osborne and Miss Sedley, and the pair, smiling wryly, looked at Rebecca, who actually blushed as she folded her blonde curls over her knitting. How his heart beat when Joseph appeared - Joseph, blowing off the stairs in shiny, creaking boots - Joseph, in a new waistcoat, red with heat and nervousness, and blushing behind his hooded scarf. It was a nervous moment for all; and as for Amelia, I think she was more scared than even the people most concerned.

Sambo, who opened the door and announced Mr. Joseph, followed smilingly behind the collector, carrying two beautiful bouquets of flowers, which the monster had had the gallantry to buy at the Covent Garden market this that morning - they weren't as big as the haystacks that the ladies carry with them today, in cones of watermarked paper; but the young women were delighted with the gift, for Joseph offered one to each, with extremely solemn reverence.

" Well done Jos ! " Cried Osborne.

- Thank you, dear Joseph, said Amélie, all ready to kiss her brother, if he wanted to. (And I think for a kiss from a creature as dear as Amelia, I would buy all of Mr. Lee's verandas right away.)

" O heavenly flowers, heavenly ! " Exclaimed Miss Sharp, and felt gently, and pressed against his chest, and looked up at the ceiling, in an ecstasy of admiration. Perhaps she first looked in the bouquet, to see if there was a sweet note hidden among the flowers; but there was no letter.

" Do they speak the language of flowers to Boggley Wollah, Sedley ?" " Asked Osborne laughed.

" Pooh , nonsense ! " Said the sentimental youth. " I bought them from Nathan ; very glad that you like them ; and hey, Amelia, my dear, I bought a pineapple at the same time, which I gave to Sambo. Take it for tiffin ; very cool and fun hot weather. " Rebecca said she had never tasted a pine, and yearned above all to taste one.

So the conversation continued. I don't know under what pretext Osborne left the room, or why, soon, Amelia left, perhaps to supervise the slicing of the pineapple; but Jos was left alone with Rebecca, who had resumed her work, and the green silk and the shining needles were trembling rapidly under her thin, white fingers.

"What a beautiful BYOO-OOTIFUL song you sang last night, dear Miss Sharp," the collector said. "It almost made me cry; 'pon my honor, he did."

" Because you have a good heart, Mr. Joseph ; all Sedleys have them, I think. "

"It kept me awake last night, and I was trying to hum it this morning, in bed; I was, on my honor. Gollop, my doctor, came at eleven o'clock (for I'm a sad cripple, you know, and seeing Gollop every day), and, ' god! I was there, singing like ... a robin.'

"O funny creature! Let me hear you sing it.

"Me? No, you, Miss Sharp; my dear Miss Sharp, sing it." "Not now, Mr. Sedley," Rebecca said, with a sigh. "My spirits are not up to the task; besides, I have to finish the scholarship. Will you help me, Mr. Sedley? And before he had time to ask how, Mr. Joseph Sedley, of the East India Company service, was actually sitting one-on-one with a young woman, looking at her with a most murderous expression. ; her arms stretched out before her in a pleading attitude, and her hands were tied in a green silk cloth which she unrolled.

In this romantic position, Osborne and Amelia found the couple interesting when they entered to announce that Tiffin was ready. The silk skein had just been wrapped around the card; but M. Jos had never spoken.

"I 'm sure he will do it tonight, my dear," Amelia said, as she shook Rebecca's hand; and Sedley, too, had communicated with her soul, and thought to herself, "'Gad, I'm going to ask Vauxhall."

CHAPTER V
Dobbin of ours

Cuff's fight with Dobbin and the unexpected outcome of this contest will long be remembered by all men who were educated at the famous school of Dr. Swishtail. This latter youngster (formerly called Heigh-ho Dobbin, Gee-ho Dobbin, and by many other names indicative of childish contempt) was the quietest, most awkward, and, as it seemed, the most boring of all. all of Dr. Swishtail's youngsters. Gentlemen. His parents were grocers in town: and it was rumored that he had been admitted to Dr Swishtail's academy on what are called "mutual principles", that is to say that the expenses of his pension and of his schooling was paid by his father in goods, not money ; and he stood there - mostly at the back of the school - in his corduroys and jacket, through the seams of which his big bones were bursting - like the representative of so many pounds of tea, candles, sugar , marbled soap, plums (a very small proportion of which was provided for the establishment's puddings), and other commodities. A terrible day it was for young Dobbin when one of the kids at school, having run into town on a hardbake and polonies poaching excursion, spotted the cart of Dobbin & Rudge, Grocers and Oilmen , Thames Street, London, at Doctor's Door, unloading a cargo of the goods the company was handling.

Young Dobbin had no peace after that. The jokes were frightening and ruthless against him. "Hello, Dobbin," a joker would say, "here's some good news in the paper. Sugars are at risk, my boy." Another would fix a sum: "If a pound of sheep candles costs seven cents, how much must Dobbin cost?" and a roar would ensue from the whole circle of young rascals, usher and all, who rightly considered the retailing of merchandise a shameful and infamous practice, deserving the contempt and contempt of all true gentlemen.

"Your father is just a merchant, Osborne," Dobbin said privately to the little boy who had brought the storm down on him. To which the latter replied haughtily: "My father is a gentleman and keeps his car"; and Mr. William Dobbin retired to a remote outbuilding in the playground, where he spent a half-vacation in the most bitter sadness and misfortune. Who among us does not remember such hours of bitter and bitter childhood grief ? Who feels injustice; which shrinks before an affront; who has such a keen sense of evil, and such dazzling gratitude for kindness, like a generous boy? and how many of those sweet souls do you degrade, move away, torture yourself, because of a little cowardly calculation and a miserable Latin dog?

Now William Dobbin, from an inability to acquire the rudiments of the above language as offered in this wonderful book Eton's Latin Grammar, has been forced to remain among the very last scholars of Doctor Swishtail. , and was continually "pulled out" by little ones with pink faces and aprons as he stepped forward with the low form, a giant among them, with his dejected and stunned look, his flayed bait and tight corduroys. High and low, everyone laughed at him. They sewed these corduroys, no matter how tight they were. They cut the strings of his bed. They knocked over buckets and benches, so he could break his shins on them, which he never failed to do. Packages were sent to him which, when opened, contained the father's soap and candles. There was no little guy but had his taunt and joke in Dobbin; and he endured it all patiently enough, and was entirely mute and miserable.

Cuff, on the contrary, was the great leader and dandy of Swishtail Seminary. He smuggled wine. He fought the bourgeoisie. The ponies would pick him up to go home on Saturday. He had his boots in his room, where he hunted during the holidays. He had a gold repeater : and prized like the Doctor. He had been to the Opera and knew the merits of the main actors, preferring Mr. Kean to Mr. Kemble. It could knock you down forty Latin verses in an hour. He could do French poetry. What else didn't he know, or could he do? They said even the Doctor himself was afraid of him.

Cuff, the undisputed king of the school, ruled and intimidated his subjects with splendid superiority. This one darkened his shoes: it made his bread toast, others homed, and gave him cricket balls all summer afternoon. "Figs " was the individual he despised the most, and with whom, though he still cursed and laughed at him, he barely deigned to have a personal communication.

One day in private, the two young gentlemen had had a difference. Figs, alone in the classroom, blundered over a family letter ; when Cuff, entering, tells him to go over to some message, of which the pies were probably the subject.

"I can't," said Dobbin; "I want to finish my letter.

" You CAN'T ? " Says Mr. Cuff, entering this document (in which many words were removed, many were misspelled, which was spent umpteen reflection, and work, and tears, for the poor boy was writing to her mother, who loved her, although she was a grocer's wife and lived in a back salon on Thames Street). " You CAN'T ? " Says Mr. Cuff," I want to know why, I beg you? Can't you write old mother Figs tomorrow?

"Don't shout names," Dobbin said, coming off the bench very nervous.

" Well , sir, would you like to go ? " Crowed the cock of the school.

" Put down the letter, " Dobbin replied ; "no gentleman readth letterth."

"Well, NOW are you going to go?" said the other.

"No, I won't. Don't hit, or I'll crush you," Dobbin roared, rushing towards a lead inkwell, and looking so mean, that Mr. Cuff stopped, lowered again. the sleeves of his coat, put his hands in his pockets, and walked away with a sneer. But he never personally meddled with the grocer's boy after that; although we owe him justice to say that he always spoke of Mr. Dobbin with contempt behind his back.

Some time after this interview it happened that Mr. Cuff, on a sunny afternoon, was in the neighborhood of poor William Dobbin, who was lying under a tree in the playground, spelling out a favorite copy of the Thousand and One. nights he had apart. the rest of the school, who practiced their various sports, quite alone and almost happy. If people wanted to leave the children to themselves; if teachers stopped bullying them; if parents did not insist on directing their thoughts and dominating their feelings - those feelings and thoughts that are a mystery to all (for how much you and I know each other, our children, our fathers, our neighbor, and how likely are the thoughts of the poor boy or the poor girl you rule to be more beautiful and sacred than those of the dull and corrupt person who rules it?) - if, I say, the parents and the teachers left their children alone a little more, a little harm would accumulate, although a lesser amount of as in praesenti could be acquired.

Well, William Dobbin had for once forgotten the world, and had left with Sindbad the Sailor in the Valley of Diamonds, or with Prince Ahmed and the Fairy Peribanou in this lovely cave where the Prince found her, and where we would all love to pay a visit; when shrill cries, like a little man in tears, awoke his sweet reverie; and looking up he saw Cuff in front of him, manhandling a little boy.

It was the boy who had caught him about the grocer's cart; but he bore little wickedness, not at least towards the young and the little ones. " How dare you, sir, break the bottle ?" " Says Cuff to the little boy swinging above him a strain of yellow cricket.

The boy had been ordered to cross the wall of the playing field (at a chosen spot where the broken glass had been removed from the top and from the niches made in the brick) ; run a quarter mile; buy a pint of rum on credit; brave all the spies away from the Doctor and return to the playground again; during the accomplishment of this feat, his foot had slipped, and the bottle had shattered, and the shrub had been knocked down, and his pants had been damaged, and he appeared before his employer as a perfectly guilty and trembling wretch, albeit harmless.

" How dare you, sir, break it ?" " Said cuff; you drank the shrub, and now you claim to have broken the bottle. Hold your hand, sir.

The stump fell with a loud thud on the child's hand. A moan followed. Dobbin looked up. The fairy Peribanou had fled into the most secret cave with Prince Ahmed: the Rock had taken Sindbad the sailor out of sight of the Valley of Diamonds, far in the clouds: and that was everyday life before the honest Guillaume; and a big boy beating a little one for no reason.

" Hold out your other hand, sir, " Cuff roared to his little schoolmate, whose face was contorted with pain. Dobbin shivered and gathered in his old tight clothes.

"Take that, little devil!" cried Mr. Cuff, and the wicket fell back into the child's hand. - Don't be horrified, ladies, all the boys in a public school did. Your children will and in all likelihood will. The wicket went down again; and Dobbin started up.

I can't say what his motive was. Torture in a public school is as much permitted as knout in Russia. He wouldn't be a gentleman (in a way) to resist her. Perhaps Dobbin's mad soul revolted against this exercise of tyranny; or maybe he had a burning desire for revenge in his mind and he wanted to measure himself against this splendid tyrant and tyrant, who had all the glory, pride, pomp, circumstance, flying banners, drums beating, guards saluting, in the square. Whatever his motivation, however, he jumped up and yelled, " Wait, Cuff ; no longer bully this child ; where I am going— "

"Or what do you want ? " Cuff asked in amazement at the interruption. "Hold out your hand, little beast.

"I'm going to give you the worst beating you've ever had in your life," Dobbin said, responding to the first part of Cuff's sentence; and little Osborne, panting and in tears, looked up in astonishment and disbelief as he saw this astonishing champion suddenly rise up to defend him: while Cuff's astonishment was no less. Imagine our late monarch George III when he heard of the North American Colonial Uprising : imagine Goliath cheeky when little David stepped forward and called for a meeting; and you have the feelings of Mr. Reginald Cuff when this meeting was proposed to him.

"After school," he said, "of course; after a pause and a look, you might as well say: "Make your will, and communicate your last wishes to your friends between this hour and that one."

"As you want," Dobbin said. "You must be my bottle holder, Osborne.

"Well, if you like," replied little Osborne; because you see that his daddy was running a car, and he was a little ashamed of his champion.

Yes, when the hour for battle came he was almost ashamed to say, "Go on, Figs"; and not a single other boy in the place uttered this cry during the first two or three rounds of this famous fight; at the beginning of which the scientist Cuff, with a contemptuous smile on his face, and as light and as gay as if he were at the ball, planted his blows on his adversary, and defeated this unfortunate champion three times in a row. With each fall there was a cheer; and everyone wanted to have the honor of offering a knee to the winner.

What a lick I'll have when this is over, thought young Osborne as he picked up his man. "You better give in," he said to Dobbin; "It's just a beating, Figs, and you know I'm used to it." But Figs, whose limbs were all trembling and whose nostrils breathed rage, pushed aside his little bottle holder and entered a fourth time.

Since he had no idea how to parry his punches, and Cuff had started the attack the three previous times, never allowing his enemy to strike, Figs then decided he would start the engagement with a charge on his part; and accordingly, being a left-handed man, put that arm into action, and struck two or three times with all his might, once at Mr. Cuff's left eye, and once upon his handsome Roman nose.

The headline went down this time, to the amazement of the assembly. "Nice hit, by Jove," said little Osborne, with the air of a connoisseur, patting his man on the back. "Give it to him with the left, Figs my boy."

Figs' left made a terrific play for the rest of the fight. The armband fell off every time. In the sixth round, there were almost as many guys shouting " Go -y, Figs ," there were young exclaiming : " Go on, Cuff ." In the twelfth round, this last champion was all abroad, as they say, and had lost all presence of mind and all power of attack or defense. Figs, on the contrary, was as calm as a Quaker. His face being quite pale, his bright eyes open, and a large cut on his lower lip bleeding profusely, gave this young man a fierce and horrible look, which perhaps struck terror in many onlookers. Nevertheless, his intrepid opponent was about to close for the thirteenth time.

If I had the pen of a Napier, or a Bell's Life, I would like to describe this fight. It was the last charge of the Guard - (that is to say it would have been, only Waterloo had not yet taken place) - it was the column of Ney enclosing the hill of the Hague Sainte, bristling with ten thousand bayonets and crowned with twenty eagles - it was the cry of the beef-eating Britons, as, leaping from the hill, they rushed to embrace the enemy in the savage arms of battle - in others In terms, Cuff arrived brave enough, but quite tottering and groggy, the Fig- the

Merchant put his left as usual on his opponent's nose, and let him down one last time.

"I think that will suit him," said Figs, as his opponent fell so cleanly on the green that I saw Jack Spot's ball sink into the pool's pocket ; and the point is that when the time was called Mr. Reginald Cuff could not, or did not choose, to rise again.

And now all the boys have made such a cry for Figs that you would have thought he had been their cherished champion the whole battle; and as absolutely pulled Dr. Swishtail out of his study, curious to know the cause of the uproar. He threatened to violently whip Figs, of course; but Cuff, who had come to himself by then and was washing his wounds, stood up and said, "It's my fault, sir, not Figs, not Dobbin's." I was bullying a little boy and he served me well. " By what magnanimous speech he not only spared his conqueror a lash, but regained all his influence over the boys his defeat had nearly cost him.

Young Osborne wrote his parents an account of the transaction.

Sugar Cane House, Richmond, March 18 -

Dear mom, I hope you are doing well. I would be grateful if you could send me a cake and five shillings. There was a fight here between Cuff and Dobbin. Cuff, you know, was the school rooster. They fought thirteen rounds, and Dobbin licked it. So Cuff is now Only Second Cock. The fight was about me. Cuff was licking me for breaking a bottle of milk, and Figs couldn't stand it. We call him Figs because his father is a grocer — Figs & Rudge, Thames St., City — I think he fought for me, you should buy your tea and sugar from his father. Cuff comes home every Saturday, but he can't because he has 2 black eyes. He has a white pony to pick him up, and a livery groom on a bay mare. I wish my daddy would let me have a pony, and I am

Your devoted son, GEORGE SEDLEY
OSBORNE

PS — Give my love to little Emmy. I cut a
Coach out of cardboard for him. Please, not
a seed cake, but a plum cake.

Following Dobbin's victory, his character rose prodigiously in the
esteem of all his schoolmates, and the name Figs, which had been a
synonym of reproach, became such a respectable and popular
nickname as n any other in use in the school. "After all, it's not his
fault that his father is a grocer," said George Osborne, who, although
a small guy, was very popular among the young Swishtail; and his
opinion was received with great applause. It was voted down to make
fun of Dobbin about this birth accident. "Old Figs" has become a name
of kindness and affection; and the slyness of a bailiff no longer
laughcd at him.

And Dobbin's spirit soared with his changed circumstances. He
has made wonderful progress in learning at school. The superb Cuff
himself, at whose condescension Dobbin could only blush and marvel,
helped him continue his Latin verses ; "coachcd" him during playing
hours: carried him triumphantly from the class of small boys of
avcragc shapc; and even there was a just place for him. It was found
that, although dull in classical learning, he was exceptionally fast in
mathematics. To everyone's satisfaction, he passed third in algebra
and obtained a prize book in French for the public examination of the
summer solstice. You should have seen his mother's face when
Telemachus (that delicious romance) was presented to him by the
Doctor in front of the whole school and parents and company, with an
inscription in Gulielmo Dobbin. All the boys clapped in applause and
sympathy. His blushes, his stumbles, his clumsiness, and the number
of feet he crushed in regaining his place, who will describe
or calculate? Old Dobbin, his father, who now respected him for the
first time, publicly gave him two guineas; most of which he spent in a
general shed for school; and he came back in tail after the
holidays.

Dobbin was a young man far too modest to suppose that this happy change in all his circumstances came from his own generous and manly disposition: he chose, out of perversity, to attribute his good fortune to the agency alone and to the benevolence of the little one. George Osborne, to whom he now devoted a love and affection that only children feel, such affection , as we read in the charming fairy book, that the rude Orson had for the splendid young Valentine his conqueror. He threw himself at little Osborne's feet and loved him. Before they even knew each other, he had admired Osborne in secret. Now he was her valet, her dog, her man on Friday. He believed that Osborne had all the perfections, was the most beautiful, the bravest, the most active, the most intelligent, the most generous of the boys created. He shared his money with him: bought him countless gifts of knives, pencil cases, gold seals, caramel, little warblers and romantic books, with large colorful images of knights and thieves, in most of which you might read inscriptions to George Sedley Osborne, squire, from his attached friend William Dobbin - testimonies of homage which George received most graciously, as he became his superior merit.

So Lieutenant Osborne, coming to Russell Square on Vauxhall's feast day, said to the ladies : ' Mrs. Sedley, ma'am, I hope you have room ; I asked Dobbin to come and have dinner here. , and go with us to Vauxhall. He is almost as modest as Jos. "

" The modesty ! Puoh, " said the fat gentleman, giving Miss Sharp a victorious look.

"He is ... but you are incomparably more graceful, Sedley," Osborne added, laughing. "I met him at Bedford when I went to get you; and I told her that Miss Amelia was back home, and we were all determined to go out for a night of fun; and that Mrs. Sedley had forgiven his breakup. the bowl of punch at the children's party. Don't you remember the disaster, ma'am, seven years ago?

"Over Mrs. Flamingo's crimson silk dress," said Mrs. Sedley cheerfully. "What was weird! And her sisters aren't much more gracious. Lady Dobbin was in Highbury last night with three of them. Such figures! My darlings."

"The alderman is very rich, isn't he?" Osborne said mischievously. "Do n't you think one of the girls would be a good specialty for me, ma'am?"

"You foolish creature! Who would take you, I would like to know, with your yellow face ?

" Mine a yellow face ?" Stop until you see Dobbin. Now, he's had yellow fever three times ; twice in Nassau and once in St. Kitts. "

"Good , good, yours is pretty yellow for us." Isn't it, Emmy? Mrs. Sedley said: at what speech Miss Amelia only made a smile and blush; and looking at the pale and interesting face of Mr. George Osborne, and those beautiful black, curly and shiny mustaches, which the young man himself regarded without ordinary complacency, she thought in her little heart that in His Majesty's army , or in the wide world, there has never been such a face or such a hero. "I do n't care about Captain Dobbin's complexion," she said, "or how awkward he is. I will always love him, I know that, " his small reason being that he was George's friend and champion.

"There isn't a better guy in the service," Osborne said, "nor a better officer, although he's not an Adonis, sure." And he himself looked towards the glass with much naivety; and, in doing so, she caught Miss Sharp's eye on him, to which he blushed a little, and Rebecca thought in her heart: " Ah, my handsome sir !" I think I have YOUR gauge " - the cunning little rascal !

That evening, when Amelia stumbled into the living room in a white muslin gown, prepared for the conquest at Vauxhall, singing like a lark and as fresh as a rose - a very tall, unsightly gentleman, with big hands and big feet, and big ears, highlighted by shaved black hair and dressed in the dreadful military frog and bicorn coat of that time, came up to meet him and made it one of the most common bows. clumsy never performed by a mortal.

It was none other than Captain William Dobbin, of His Majesty's infantry regiment, returned from yellow fever, in the West Indies, to whom the fortune of the service had ordered his regiment, while so many of his valiant comrades reap glory in the Peninsula.

He had arrived with such a timid and silent blow that it was inaudible to the ladies upstairs: otherwise, you can be sure that Miss

Amelia would never have had the audacity to come and sing in the room. As it was, the sweet little fresh voice went straight to the captain's heart and snuggled up there. When she held out her hand for him to squeeze, before he wrapped it in his own, he stopped and thought, " Well, is that possible ... are you the little girl?" that I remember in a pink dress, such a short time ago ? the night I upset the punch bowl, right after it was published in the Gazette ? Are you the little girl George Osborne said she should marry him ? What a blossoming young creature you seem, and what a prize the thug got ! " All this, he thought, before taking the hand of Amelia in his, and dropping his cocked hat.

His story since he left school, until the very moment when we have the pleasure of finding him, although not fully told, has still, I think, been sufficiently indicated for an ingenious reader by the conversation of the last page. Dobbin, the despised grocer, was Alderman Dobbin — Alderman Dobbin was Colonel of the City Light Horse, then burning with military ardor to resist the French invasion. The body of Colonel Dobbin, in which old Mr. Osborne himself was only an indifferent corporal, had been reviewed by the Sovereign and the Duke of York; and the colonel and the alderman had been ennobled. His son had entered the army: and young Osborne soon followed him in the same regiment. They had served in the West Indies and Canada. Their regiment had just returned home, and Dobbin's attachment to George Osborne was as warm and generous now as it had been when the two were school children.

These good people therefore sat down to dinner. They spoke of war and glory, of Boney and Lord Wellington, and of the last Gazette. In those famous days, every gazette had a victory in it, and the two gallant young men desired to see their names on the glorious list, and cursed their miserable fate of belonging to a regiment which had been far from the chances of honor. Miss Sharp lit up with this exciting conversation, but Miss Sedley shivered and passed out upon hearing it. Mr. Jos told several of his tiger hunting stories, finished the one on Miss Cutler and Lance the Surgeon; helped Rebecca to put everything on the table, and he himself swallowed and drank a lot.

He sprang to open the door for the ladies, when they retired, with the most murderous grace - and, returning to the table, filled himself bumper after bumper with burgundy, which he swallowed with nervous swiftness.

"He's getting ready," Osborne whispered to Dobbin, and finally the time and car arrived for Vauxhall.

CHAPTER VI
Opel

I know the tune I'm playing is very sweet (although there are some great chapters coming up right now), and I must beg the good-natured reader to remember that we are currently only talking about a family of stockbroker in Russell Square, walking around, or having lunch, or having dinner, or talking and making love as people do in common life, and without a single passionate and wonderful incident to mark the progress of their love affairs. The argument is so - Osborne, Amelia's lover, invited an old friend to dinner and to Vauxhall - Jos Sedley is in love with Rebecca. Will he marry her ? This is the big topic at hand.

We could have treated this subject in a distinguished, or romantic, or facetious manner. Suppose we set the scene in Grosvenor Square, with the same adventures, wouldn't some people have listened? Suppose we have shown how Lord Joseph Sedley fell in love, and the Marquis of Osborne became attached to Lady Amelia, with the full consent of the Duke, her noble father: or instead of the extremely distinguished, suppose that we resorted to utterly low, and described what was going on in Mr. Sedley's kitchen - how black Sambo was in love with the cook (as he was for that matter), and how he got down to it. beaten with the coachman in his favor; how the cutler was caught stealing a cold shoulder of mutton, and Miss Sedley's new maid refused to go to bed without a wax candle; such incidents could provoke a lot of delicious laughter and be supposed to represent scenes of "life". Or if, on the contrary, we had developed a taste for the terrible, and made the lover of the new maid a professional burglar, who bursts into the house with his gang, slaughters the black Sambo at his master's feet, and Taking Amélie in a nightgown, not to let go until the third volume, we could easily have built a story of palpitating interest, through the fiery chapters which the reader would hasten, panting. But my readers should not hope for such romance, only a simple story, and should be content with a chapter on Vauxhall, which is so short that it hardly deserves to be called a chapter. And yet, it is a chapter, and very important too. Are there not small chapters in everyone's life that seem to be nothing, yet affect the rest of the story?

Then let's get on the bus with the Russell Square party and go to the gardens. There's barely room between Jos and Miss Sharp, who are in the front seat. Mr. Osborne seated opposite, between Captain Dobbin and Amelia.

Every soul in the car agreed that that night Jos would offer to make Rebecca Sharp Mrs. Sedley. The parents at home had agreed to the arrangement, however, between us old Mr. Sedley had a very close feeling of contempt for his son. He said he was conceited, selfish, lazy and effeminate. He couldn't stand his fashionable airs and laughed heartily at his pompous boasting. "I will leave to the comrade half of my property," he said; "And he will have, besides, a lot of his own; but how I am perfectly sure that if you, and I, and his sister were to die tomorrow, he would say "God damn it!" and eat his dinner as well as usual, I'm not going to worry about him. Let him marry whomever he wants. This is not my business.

Amelia, on the other hand, as a young lady of her prudence and temperament, was pretty excited about the match. Once or twice Jos had been about to say something very important to her, which she was very willing to listen to, but the big one could not be made to reveal his great secret, and much to that of his sister. Disappointment, he only let go of a big sigh and turned away.

This mystery served to keep Amelia's soft chest in a perpetual movement of excitement. If she did not speak with Rebecca on the delicate subject, she made up for it by long and intimate conversations with Mrs. Blenkinsop, the housekeeper, who left some clues for the maid, who had perhaps briefly brought up the matter to the cook. , which carried the news, I have no doubt, to all traders, so that the marriage of Mr. Jos has now been spoken of by a very considerable number of people in the world of Russell Square.

It was, of course, Mrs. Sedley's opinion that her son would demean himself by marriage to an artist's daughter. "But, lor ', madam," ejaculated Mrs. Blenkinsop, "we were just grocers when we married MS, who was a stockbroker, and we didn't have five hundred pounds with us, and we I am rich enough now. " And Amelia was entirely of this opinion, to which, gradually, the good humor Mrs. Sedley was brought.

Mr. Sedley was neutral. " Let Jos marry whoever he wants, " he said ; "It's none of my business. This girl has no fortune; neither is Mrs. Sedley. She seems cheerful and intelligent, and maybe will keep it tidy. Better her, my dear, than a Mrs. Black Sedley, and a dozen mahogany grandchildren. "

So that everything seemed to smile on Rebecca's fortune. She naturally took Jos' arm as she went to dinner; she had sat next to him on the body of his uncovered car (a most formidable "male" that he was, as he sat there, serene, in good shape, driving his grays), and although no one hadn't said a word about the wedding, everyone seemed to understand that. All she wanted was the proposal, and ah! how Rebecca now felt the need for a mother! - a dear and tender mother, who would have managed the affair in ten minutes, and, during a small confidential and delicate conversation, would have extracted the interesting confession from the shy lips of the young man!

This was the situation when the car crossed Westminster Bridge.

The party landed at the Royal Gardens in due course. As the majestic Jos exited the squeaky vehicle, the crowd applauded the fat gentleman, who blushed and looked very tall and powerful, as he walked away with Rebecca under his arm. George, of course, took charge of Amelia. She looked as happy as a rosebush in the sun.

" I say, Dobbin, " said George, " just look at the shawls and stuff, there's a good guy. " And so, as he teamed with Miss Sedley and Jos crept through the gate of the gardens with Rebecca at his side, the honest Dobbin contented himself with one arm shawls and pay at the door for all Party.

He walked very modestly behind them. He didn't want to spoil the sport. About Rebecca and Jos, he didn't care. But he thought Amelia was worthy even of the brilliant George Osborne, and as he saw this beautiful couple donning the walks for the maiden's delight and wonder, he looked at her naive bliss with a sort of fatherly delight. Maybe he felt he wished he had something on his own arm besides a shawl (people laughed when they saw the lanky young officer carrying this female burden); but William Dobbin was very little addicted to selfish calculations; and as long as his friend was having fun, how would he be unhappy? And the truth is that of all the delights of the Gardens; a hundred thousand additional lamps, which were always on; the fiddlers in bicornuate, playing lovely melodies under the golden hull in the middle of the gardens; the singers, both comic and sentimental ballads, which charmed the ears; country dances, formed by bouncy cockneys and cockneyesses, and performed amid jumps, kicks and laughter; the signal announcing that Madame Saqui was going to ascend towards the sky on a soft rope ascending towards the stars; the hermit who always sat in the illuminated hermitage; the gloomy walks, so conducive to conversations with young lovers; the pots of stout handed out by the people in the dingy old liveries; and the glittering boxes, in which the merry feasts pretended to eat almost invisible slices of ham, of all those things, and of the kind Simpson, that amiable smiling idiot, who, dare I say it, already presided over the place. ... William Dobbin does not pay the slightest attention to it.

He wore Amelia's white cashmere shawl, and having attended under the golden shell, while Mrs. Salmon performed the Battle of Borodino (a savage cantata against the Corsican upstart, who had recently encountered his Russian setbacks) - Mr. Dobbin tried to hum it as she walked away and found it humming - the tune Amelia Sedley was singing on the stairs, as she came down to dinner.

He burst out laughing at himself ; for the truth is, he couldn't sing better than an owl.

It goes without saying that our young people, being in groups of two and two, made the most solemn promises to keep together during the evening, and parted ten minutes later. The parties at Vauxhall always went their separate ways, but it was only to meet again at supper time, when they could talk about their mutual adventures in the meantime.

What were the adventures of Mr. Osborne and Miss Amelia? It's a secret. But know it well, they were perfectly happy and correct in their conduct; and as they had been used to being together for fifteen years, their tete-a-tete offered no particular novelty.

But when Miss Rebecca Sharp and her sturdy companion got lost on a lonely walk, in which there were no more than five dozen couples straying alike, they both felt the situation was extremely tender and critical, and now or never was Miss Thought High, to elicit that statement which quivered on Mr. Sedley's timid lips. They had already been to the Moscow Panorama, where a rude man, stepping on Miss Sharp's foot, let her fall back with a little piercing cry into Mr. Sedley's arms, and this little incident increased the tenderness and confidence of this man. gentleman. to the point that he told her several of her favorite Indian stories at least for the sixth time.

"How I would love to see India! said Rebecca.

"Should you?" said Joseph with the most murderous tenderness; and was no doubt about to follow this artful interrogation with an even more tender question (for he huffed and panted a lot, and Rebecca's hand, which was placed near his heart, could count the feverish pulsations of this organ.), when, oh, provoking! the bell rang for the fireworks display, and, with a great brawl and a great race taking place, these interesting lovers were forced to follow the flood of people.

Captain Dobbin considered joining the party at supper: as, in truth, he found the Vauxhall amusements not particularly lively, but he paraded twice in front of the lodge where the now-united couples gathered, and no one paid attention to him. . Blankets were laid for four. The mated couples chatted happily, and Dobbin knew he was as completely forgotten as if he had never existed in this world.

"I should only be too many," said the captain, looking at them rather wistfully. " I 'd better go talk to the hermit, " - and so he moved away from the hum of men, the noise and the din of the banquet, down the dark alley, at the end of which lived that famous Solitaire box. It wasn't much fun for Dobbin - and, indeed, being alone in Vauxhall, I have found, in my own experience, to be one of the most gloomy sports a bachelor has ever played.

The two couples were then perfectly happy in their dressing room: where the most delicious and intimate conversation took place. Jos was in his glory, commanding the waiters with great majesty. He made the salad; and uncorked the Champagne; and carved the chickens; and ate and drank most of the refreshments on the tables. Finally, he insisted on having a bowl of punch rack; everyone had punch at Vauxhall. " Waiter , punch. "

That punch rack bowl was the cause of this whole thing. And why not a punch rack bowl as well as any other cause? Wasn't a bowl of prussic acid the cause of Fair Rosamond's retirement from the world? Wasn't a bowl of wine the cause of Alexander the Great's disappearance, or at least Dr. Lemprière didn't say so? a hero, "which we now relate. It influenced their lives, although most of them haven't tasted a drop of it.

The young ladies did not drink it; Osborne didn't like it; and the consequence was that Jos, this big greedy, drank all the contents of the bowl; and the consequence of his drinking the entire contents of the bowl was a liveliness which at first was astonishing, then became almost painful; for he was talking and laughing so loudly that he drew dozens of listeners around the lodge, much to the confusion of the innocent party there; and, volunteering to sing a song (which he did in that tearful tone peculiar to drunken gentlemen), he almost dragged the audience which had gathered around the musicians in the golden shell, and received from his listeners a lot of applause.

" Brayvo , big one !" " Said one; "Angcore, Daniel Lambert! said another; "What a number for the tightrope!" cried another joke, to the inexpressible alarm of the ladies, and to the great anger of Mr. Osborne.

"For heaven's sake, Jos, let's get up and go," cried this gentleman, and the young women stood up.

" Stop , my dear diddle-diddle-darling, " cried Jos, now as bold as a lion, and hugging Miss Rebecca around the waist. Rebecca jumped, but she couldn't remove her hand. The laughter redoubled outside. Jos continued to drink, make love and sing; and, winking and gracefully waving his glass at his audience, challenged all or part to come in and take a share of his punch.

Mr. Osborne was about to run over a gentleman in ankle boots, who proposed to take advantage of this invitation, and a commotion seemed inevitable, when by the greatest luck a gentleman by the name of Dobbin, who had strolled through the gardens , walked towards the lodge. "Go ahead , fools! said this gentleman, pushing aside a large number of the crowd which soon disappeared before his cocked hat and his fierce air, and he entered the box in the most agitated state.

"Good God! Dobbin, where have you been? Osborne said, grabbing the white cashmere shawl from his friend's arm and snuggling Amelia into it. - Make yourself useful and take care of Jos here, while I take the ladies in the car.

Jos was ready to stand up to interfere, but a simple push of Osborne's finger sent him back into his seat, and the lieutenant was able to safely remove the ladies. Jos kissed their hand as they pulled out and hiccupped " Blessed be you!" Then, seizing the hand of Captain Dobbin, and weeping in the most pitiful manner, he confided to this gentleman the secret of his loves. He adored this girl who had just come out; he had broken his heart, he knew, by his conduct; he would marry her the next morning in St. George's, Hanover Square; he would overthrow the Archbishop of Canterbury in Lambeth: he would do it, by Jupiter! and have it ready; and, acting on this indication, Captain Dobbin shrewdly urged him to leave the gardens and rush towards Lambeth Palace, and, once out of the gates, easily transported Mr. Jos Sedley in a cab-coach, which l 'deposited safely at his accommodation.

George Osborne led the girls home safely: and when the door was closed on them, and as he walked through Russell Square, he laughed so as to astonish the keeper. Amelia looked at her friend very sadly as they walked up the stairs, kissed her and lay down without speaking.

"He has to propose tomorrow," Rebecca thought. "He called me the darling of his soul, four times; he shook my hand in Amélie's presence. He has to propose tomorrow. And that's what Amelia thought too. And I dare say that she thought about the dress she was to wear as a bridesmaid, and the gifts she would give to her sweet little sister-in-law, and a subsequent ceremony in which she herself could play a leading role, & c. , and & c., and & c., and & c.

ignorant young creatures! As you know little about the effect of the punch rack ! What is the rack in the punch at night, in the rack in the head of a morning? To this truth, I can testify as a man; there is no headache in the world like the one caused by the Vauxhall punch. In twenty years, I remember the consequence of two drinks! two wine glasses! but two, on the honor of a gentleman; and Joseph Sedley, who had liver disease, had swallowed at least a liter of the abominable mixture.

The next morning, which Rebecca thought was on the cusp of her fortune, Sedley was moaning in anguish the pen refuses to describe. Sparkling water has not yet been invented. The small beer - one would believe ! - was the only drink the unfortunate gentlemen soothe the fever of their potation the night before. With that sweet drink in front of him, George Osborne found Boggley Wollah's ex-collector moaning on the couch in his apartment. Dobbin was already in the room, kindly tending to his patient from the night before . The two officers, looking at the prostrate Bacchanalian, and looking askance at each other, exchanged the most frightening sympathetic smiles. Even Sedley's valet, the most solemn and correct of gentlemen, with the silence and gravity of an undertaker , could barely keep his face in order, looking at his hapless master.

" Mr. Sedley was unusual last night, sir, " he whispered confidently to Osborne, as the latter climbed the stairs. "He wanted to fight the 'ackney-coachman, sir. The Capting was forced to bring him upstairs in his misdeeds as a baby." A momentary smile crossed Mr. Brush's features as he spoke; Instantly, however, they fell back into their usual unfathomable calm, as he opened the living room door and announced "Mr. Hosbin."

"How are you, Sedley?" began this young prankster, after having probed his victim. "No broken bones? There's a cab driver downstairs with a black eye, and a tied head, swearing he'll rule over you.

"What do you mean by law? Sedley asked weakly.

"For beating him up last night, right, Dobbin?" You hit, sir, like Molyneux. The warden says he has never seen a man descend so straight. Ask Dobbin.

"You HAVE had a tour with the coachman," said Captain Dobbin, "and you also showed a lot of fighting."

"And that guy in the white coat in Vauxhall! How Jos ran on him! How the women screamed! By Jupiter, sir, it felt good to see you. I thought you civilians didn't had no courage; but I'll never have it in your way when you're in your cups, Jos. "

"I think I'm very terrible, when I'm awake," jos ejaculated from the couch, and made a face so sad and ridiculous, the captain's politeness couldn't hold him back, and he and Osborne fired a volley. ringing of laughter.

Osborne pursued his advantage without mercy. He thought Jos was a milksop. He had turned in his mind the question of the pending marriage between Jos and Rebecca, and was not too happy that a member of a family in which he, George Osborne, of —th, was going to marry, made a misalliance. with a little person, a little upstart housekeeper. "You knock, poor old man! Osborne said . " You are terrible ! Why, man, you couldn't stand up - you made everyone in the gardens laugh, even though you were crying yourself. You were tearful, Jos. Don't you remember singing a song ? "

"A what?" Jos asked.

"A sentimental song, and calling Rosa, Rebecca, what's her name, Amelia's girlfriend, your dearest darling?" And this ruthless young man, grabbing Dobbin's hand, acted on the stage, to the horror of the original performer, and despite Dobbin's cheerful pleas for mercy.

"Why should I spare him?" Osborne said to his friend's remonstrance, when they left the patient, leaving him in the hands of Doctor Gollop. "What's the right thing for him to be protective of himself and make a fool of us at Vauxhall?" Who is this little schoolgirl who ogles him and makes love to him? Wait, the family is low enough already, without HER. A housekeeper is fine, but I would rather have a lady for my sister-in-law. I am a liberal man, but I have pride and I know my own situation: let him know his. And I will take down this great harasser Nabob, and prevent him from being made crazier than him. That's why I told her to be careful, lest she sue him.

"I guess you know best," Dobbin said, though quite dubiously. "You have always been a curator, and your family is one of the oldest in England. But … "

"Come see the girls, and make love to Miss Sharp yourself," the lieutenant here interrupted his friend; but Captain Dobbin refused to join Osborne in his daily visit to the maidens of Russell Square.

As George walked down Southampton Row from Holborn, he laughed at the Sedley Mansion, in two different stories, seeing two heads on the prowl.

The fact is that Miss Amelia, on the balcony of the drawing-room, was looking very eagerly on the opposite side of the square, where Mr. Osborne was staying, on the lookout for the lieutenant himself ; and Miss Sharp, from her small bedroom on the second floor, was under observation until the tall form of Mr. Joseph should come into view.

"Sister Anne is at the watchtower," he said to Amélie, "but no one is coming"; and laughing and enjoying the joke hugely, he described in the most ridiculous terms to Miss Sedley, his brother's miserable condition.

"I think it's very cruel of you to laugh, George," she said, looking particularly unhappy; but George only laughed the more at his miserable and bewildered demeanor, persisted in finding the joke most entertaining, and when Miss Sharp came downstairs, mocked her very enthusiastically at the effect of her charms on the fat civilian. .

"O Miss Sharp! if you could see him this morning, he said, moaning in his flowery dressing gown, writhing on his sofa; if you could have seen him stick his tongue out at Gollop the apothecary.

" See who ? " Said Miss Sharp.

"Who ? Where ? Captain Dobbin, of course, who we were all paying attention to, by the way, last night.

"We weren't nice to him," Emmy said, blushing a lot. "I ... I completely forgot about it.

"Of course you did," Osborne cried, still laughing.

"You can't ALWAYS think about Dobbin, you know, Amelia. Is it possible, Miss Sharp?

"Except when he passed the glass of wine at dinner," said Miss Sharp, haughtily and nodded, "I never gave a single moment of consideration to the existence of Captain Dobbin."

"Alright, Miss Sharp, I'll tell her," Osborne said; and as he spoke Miss Sharp began to have a feeling of distrust and hatred towards this young officer, whom he was quite oblivious to having inspired. "He must be laughing at me, right?" Rebecca thought. " Did he make fun of me at Joseph?" Did he scare him? He may not come . " - A film passed over his eyes, and his heart beat fast.

"You're always joking," she said, smiling as innocently as she could. "All kidding aside, Mr. George; there is no one to defend ME. And George Osborne, as she walked away - and Amelia looked at him disapprovingly - felt a little manly scruple for inflicting unnecessary meanness on this helpless creature. "My dearest Amelia," he said, "you are too good, too kind. You don't know the world. I know it. And your girlfriend Miss Sharp has to learn her rank.

" Do n't you think Jos is going— "

"On my word, my dear, I don't know. He can, or not. I am not his master. I only know that he is a very stupid conceited man, and put my dear little girl in a very painful and awkward position last night. My dearest diddle-diddle- darling ! " He was laughing again, and he did it so funny that Emmy laughed too.

All day, Jos never came. But Amelia had no fear about it; for the little schemer had indeed sent the page, M. Sambo's aide-de-camp, to M. Joseph, to ask him for some book he had promised, and how he was; and the response by Jos' man, Mr. Brush, was that his master was sick in bed, and had just had the doctor with him. He's due tomorrow, she thought, but she never had the courage to tell Rebecca about it; and this young woman herself made no allusion to it during the whole evening that followed the night at Vauxhall.

The next day, however, as the two young girls were sitting on the sofa, pretending to work, write letters, or read novels, Sambo walked into the room with his usual engaging smile, a bundle under his arm and a note on a platter. " Note from Mr. Jos, miss, " said Sambo.

How Amelia trembled when she opened it!

So it ran:

> Dear Amelia, I am sending you "the orphan
> of the forest". I was too sick to come

yesterday. I'm leaving town today for Cheltenham. Please excuse me, if you can, to the kind Miss Sharp, for my conduct at Vauxhall, and beg her to forgive and forget every word I may have uttered when I was excited by this disastrous supper. As soon as I am healed, for my health is very bad, I will go to Scotland for a few months, and I am

Truly yours, Jos Sedley

It was the death warrant. It was all over. Amelia didn't dare look at Rebecca's pale face and burning eyes, but she dropped the letter on her friend's lap ; and got up, and went up to his room, and cried with all his heart.

Blenkinsop, the housekeeper, soon looked for her with consolation, on whose shoulder Amelia wept confidentially and greatly relieved herself. " Do n't beat yourself up, miss. I didn't like to tell you. But none of us in the house liked her, except at the beginning. I mourn her with my own eyes as I read your mom's letters. Pinner says she's still about you. trinket box and drawers, and everyone's drawers, and she's sure she put your white ribs in her box. "

"I gave it to her, I gave it to her," Amelia said.

But this did not change Mrs. Blenkinsop's opinion of Miss Sharp. "I don't trust those housekeepers, Pinner," she said to the maid. "They give each other the ladies' hair and hupstarts, and their pay is no better than you or me."

It was now becoming clear to all the souls in the house except poor Amelia that Rebecca should go, and high and low (always with one exception) agreed that this event should take place as soon as possible. Our good child ransacked all of her drawers, wardrobes, reticles and gadget boxes - going through all her dresses, scarves, labels, bobbins, laces, silk stockings and fallals - selecting this and that and the other, to make a little heap for Rebecca. And going to her papa's, this generous English merchant, who had promised to give her as many guineas as she had years, she begged the old gentleman to give the money to dear Rebecca, who must have been angry with it, while she lacked nothing.

She even had George Osborne contribute, and nothing loath (for he was a young man as free as any other in the military) he went to Bond Street and bought the best hat and spenser that the money can buy.

"This is George's gift to you, Rebecca, my dear," Amelia said, quite proud of the music box containing these gifts. "What a taste it tastes! There is no one like him.

"Nobody," Rebecca replied. "How grateful I am to him! She thought in her heart, "It was George Osborne who prevented my marriage. - And she loved George Osborne as a result.

She made her preparations for departure with great serenity; and accepted all of Amelia's kind gifts, after just the right amount of hesitation and reluctance. She swore eternal gratitude to Mrs. Sedley, of course; but did not impose herself too much on this good lady, who was embarrassed and obviously wanted to avoid her. She kissed Mr. Sedley's hand when he presented her with the purse; and asked for permission to consider him for the future as her good friend and protector. His demeanor was so moving that he was going to write her a check for twenty pounds more; but he was holding back his feelings: the car was waiting for him to take him to dinner, so he stumbled with a "God bless you, my dear, always come here when you come to town, you know." James. "

Finally came the parting with Miss Amelia, over which I intend to throw a veil. But after a scene where one was serious and the other a perfect performer - after the most tender caresses, the most pathetic tears, the fragrant bottle and some of the best feelings of the heart had been requisitioned - Rebecca and Amelia parted ways, the former swearing to love her friend forever.

CHAPTER VII
Crawley from Queen's Crawley

Among the most respected names beginning with C contained in the Short Guide in AD 18— were Crawley, Sir Pitt, Baronet, Great

Gaunt Street, and Queen's Crawley, Hants. This honorable name had also been constantly on the parliamentary list for many years, in conjunction with that of a number of other worthy gentlemen who took turns serving for the borough.

It is reported, as regards the Borough of Queen's Crawley, that Queen Elizabeth in one of her progress, stopping in Crawley for breakfast, was so delighted with a remarkable Hampshire beer which was brought to her then introduced by the Crawley of the day (a handsome gentleman with a cropped beard and a good leg), that she immediately erected Crawley in a borough to send two members to Parliament; and the place, from the day of that illustrious visit, took the name of Queen's Crawley, which it bears to the present day. And although, with time, and those mutations that age brought about in empires, towns and boroughs, Queen's Crawley was no longer as populous a place as it had been in the Queen's time. Bess - no, had come down to that town once called rotten - yet, as Sir Pitt Crawley would say with perfect justice in his elegant manner, "Rotten!" be hanged - that earns me well fifteen hundred dollars a year.

Sir Pitt Crawley (named after the great commoner) was the son of Walpole Crawley, First Baronet, of the Tape and Sealing-Wax Office during the reign of George II, when he was deposed for speculation, as were many other honest gentlemen of the time; and Walpole Crawley was, needless to say, the son of John Churchill Crawley, named after the famous military commander in Queen Anne's reign. The family tree (found at Queen's Crawley) further mentions Charles Stuart, later called Barebones Crawley, son of the Crawley in the time of James I; and finally, Queen Elizabeth's Crawley, who is shown in the foreground of the image with his forked beard and armor. From his waistcoat, as usual, grows a tree, on the main branches of which are inscribed the illustrious names above. Beside Sir Pitt Crawley's name Baronet (the subject of this memoir) is written that of his brother, the Reverend Bute Crawley (the great commoner was in disgrace when the Reverend Gentleman was born), rector of Crawley-cum -Snailby , and various other male and female members of the Crawley family.

Sir Pitt was first married Grizzel, sixth daughter of Mungo Binkie, Lord Binkie, and cousin, for Therefore, Mr Dundas. She brought him two sons: Pitt, named less after his father than after the heavenly born minister; and Rawdon Crawley, the friend of the Prince of Wales, whom His Majesty George IV has so completely forgotten. Many years after the death of Madame, Sir Pitt led to the altar Rosa, daughter of MG Dawson, of Mudbury, by whom he had two daughters, for whose benefit Miss Rebecca Sharp was now engaged as housekeeper. We will see that the young woman had entered a family of very distinguished relations, and was going to move in a much more distinguished circle than the one she had just left in Russell Square.

She had been ordered to join her students, in a note which was written on an old envelope, and which contained the following words :

> Sir Pitt Crawley begs Miss Sharp and the baggidge can be heard on Tuesday as I leave for Queen's Crawley tomorrow morning ERLY.

> Great Gaunt Street.

Rebecca had never seen a baronet, as far as she knew, and as soon as she had taken leave of Amelia, and counted the guineas that the good child Mr. Sedley had put in a purse for her, and soon that she had wiped her eyes with her handkerchief (an operation which she finished at the very moment when the car turned the corner of the street), she began to imagine what a baronet must be. " I wonder, is he wearing a star ?" She thought, "or is it just the lords who wear the stars?" But he will be very nicely dressed in a court costume, with ruffles, and his hair a little powdered, like Mr. Wroughton in Covent Garden. I guess he will be terribly proud, and that I will be treated with the utmost contempt. Yet I have to endure my hardship as best as I can - at least I'll be among the NICE, not the common townspeople, "and she began to think of her friends in Russell Square with that same philosophical bitterness with which , in a certain apologue, the fox is represented speaking of the grape.

After passing through Gaunt Square into Great Gaunt Street, the car finally stopped at a tall dark house between two other tall dark houses, each with a hatch above the middle living room window ; as is the custom of the houses of Great Gaunt Street, where the dreary locality seems to reign perpetually. The shutters on the first-story windows of Sir Pitt's mansion were closed, those in the dining room were partially open, and the blinds carefully covered with old newspapers.

John, the groom, who had driven the car alone, would not come down to ring the bell; and so begged a passing milkman to perform this service for him. When the bell rang, a head appeared between the interstices of the dining room shutters, and the door was opened by a man in drab breeches and gaiters, with a dirty old coat, a filthy old tie tied around his ruffled neck, a shiny bald head, a peeping red face, a pair of twinkling gray eyes, and a perpetually smiling mouth.

"That Sir Pitt Crawley's?" John said from the box.

"Ees," the man at the door said, nodding.

" Give me those 'ere trunks then, " John said.

" Hand 'n down yourself ," said the porter.

"Ca n't you see I can't leave my hoes?" Come on, give a hand, my good man, and Miss will give you some beer, " said John with a horse laugh, for he was no longer respectful to Miss Sharp, because his ties with family were severed and that she had given nothing to the servants when she left.

The bald man, taking his hands out of the pockets of his breeches, stepped forward on this summons, and throwing Miss Sharp's trunk over his shoulder, carried it into the house.

" Take this basket and this shawl, please, and open the door, " said Miss Sharp, and got out of the car with great indignation. "I will write to Mr. Sedley and inform him of your conduct," said the groom.

"Don't do it," replied the official. " I hope you haven't forgotten ? Miss Melia's dresses - do you have them - like the maid was supposed to have advertisements ? Hope they look good on you. Close the door, Jim, you won't get any profit. of 'ER,' John continued, pointing his thumb at Miss Sharp, 'a bad spell, I tell you, a bad spell,' and saying that, Mr. Sedley's groom walked away. The truth was, he was attached to the maid in question, and outraged that she had been deprived of her benefits.

.

Upon entering the dining room, on the orders of the individual in gaiters, Rebecca found that this apartment was no more cheerful than these rooms usually are, when distinguished families are out of town. The faithful chambers seem like mourning the absence of their masters. The turkey carpet has rolled up, and sulkily retreated under the sideboard: the paintings have hidden their faces behind old sheets of brown paper: the ceiling lamp is bundled up in a dismal bag of brown Holland: the curtains of the windows have disappeared under all sorts of shabby envelopes: the marble bust of Sir Walpole Crawley gazes from his dark corner at the bare boards and oiled irons, and the empty card holders above the fireplace: the cellar s' is hidden behind the carpet: the chairs are turned head and tails along the walls: and in the dark corner in front of the statue is an old-fashioned crab knife box, locked and sitting on a silent waiter.

Two kitchen chairs and a round table, and an old poker and toned-down tongs, however, were gathered around the fireplace, along with a saucepan over a weak crackling fire. There was some cheese and bread, and a pewter candlestick on the table, and a little black porter in a pint pot.

"Did you have dinner, I suppose?" Isn't it too hot for you? Like a drop of beer?

"Where's Sir Pitt Crawley?" said Miss Sharp majestically.

"He , he! I am Sir Pitt Crawley. Think you owe me a pint for dropping off your bags. He, he! Ask Tinker if I don't want to. Mrs. Tinker, Miss Sharp; Miss Governess, Mrs. Charwoman. Ho, ho! "

The lady addressed as Mrs. Tinker at this time made her appearance with a pipe and tobacco paper, for which she had been dispatched a minute before Miss Sharp's arrival ; and she handed the items to Sir Pitt, who had sat by the fire.

" Where's the farden ?" " Has he said. "I gave you three halfpence. Where's the change, old Tinker?

"The!" replied Mrs. Tinker, tossing the coin; "They're just baronets who care about farthings.

"A farthing a day is seven shillings a year," replied the deputy; "Seven shillings a year is the interest of seven guineas. Take care of your pennies, old Tinker, and your guineas will come quite natural.

"You may be sure it's Mr. Pitt Crawley, young lady," said Mrs. Tinker, sullenly; "Because he looks at his farthings. You will know him better before long."

"And like me, nothing worse, Miss Sharp," said the old man, almost polite. "I have to be fair before I am generous."

"He's never given a dime in his life," Tinker growled.

- Never, and never: it is against my principle. Go get another chair in the kitchen, Tinker, if you want to sit down; and then we'll have a little supper.

Soon the baronet plunged a fork into the saucepan on the fire, and took out of the pot a piece of tripe and an onion, which he divided into fairly equal portions, and which he shared with Mrs. Tinker. "You see, Miss Sharp, when I'm not around Tinker gets paid on board: when I'm in town she dines with the family. Haw! ah! I'm glad Miss Sharp isn't hungry, am I, Tink? " And they fell on their frugal supper.

After supper Sir Pitt Crawley began to smoke his pipe; and when it was quite dark he lit the flashlight in the pewter candlestick, and, taking out of an interminable pocket an enormous mass of papers, began to read them and put them away.

- I am here on legal matters, my dear, and that is how I will have the pleasure of such a pretty traveling companion tomorrow.

"He's still in business of the law," Ms. Tinker said, taking the porter's pot.

"Drink and drink approximately," said the baronet. " Yes ; my dear, Tinker is absolutely right : I have lost and won more cases than any man in England. Look here at Crawley, Bart. v. Snaffle. I'll knock him over, or my name is not Pitt Crawley. Podder and another against Crawley, Bart. Snaily Ward Vs Crawley, Bart. They cannot prove that it is common: I will challenge them; the earth is mine. She doesn't belong to the parish any more than she does to you or Tinker here. I will beat them, if it costs me a thousand guineas. Look at the papers; you can if you want, my dear. Do you write a good hand? I'll be of use to you when we get to Queen's Crawley, count on it, Miss Sharp. Now that the Dowager is dead, I want someone.

"She was as bad as him," Tinker said. "She took the law of each of her traders; and fired forty-eight footmen in four years."

"She was near, very near," said the baronet simply ; "but she was a valyble woman to me, and saved me a steward." - And in this confidential tension, and to the amusement of the newcomer, the conversation continued for a considerable time. Whatever qualities Sir Pitt Crawley might have, good or bad, he did not disguise them in the slightest. He talked about himself all the time, sometimes with the crudest and most vulgar accent in Hampshire; sometimes adopting the tone of a man of the world. And so, with orders for Miss Sharp to be ready at five in the morning, he wished her good night. "You will sleep with Tinker tonight," he said; "It's a king-size bed, and there's room for two. Lady Crawley died in it. Good night."

Sir Pitt walked away after this blessing, and the solemn Tinker, flashlight in hand, ascended the great dark stone staircase, through the great dreary doors of the drawing room, with the handles wrapped in paper, into the large front bedroom. , where Lady Crawley had last slept. The bed and the bedroom were so gloomy and dismal that one might have imagined not only that Lady Crawley had died in the bedroom, but that her ghost inhabited her. However, Rebecca had dashed into the apartment with the utmost vivacity, peeked into the huge wardrobes, cupboards and wardrobes, tried out the drawers that were locked, and examined the dreary pictures. and toiletries, while the old maid was praying. "I would n't like to sleep in this year-old's bed without a good conscience, mademoiselle," said the old woman. "There's room for us and a half-dozen ghosts in it," says Rebecca. "Tell me about Lady Crawley and Sir Pitt Crawley, and everyone, my DEAR Mrs. Tinker."

But old Tinker wasn't going to let this little interrogator suck him in ; and telling him that the bed was a place to sleep, not to converse, installed in his corner of the bed such a snore that only the nose of innocence can produce. Rebecca lay awake for a long, long time, thinking about the next day, and the new world she was going to, and her chances of success there. The rush light flashed in the pool. The fireplace cast a large black shadow, over half of a moldy old sampler, which his late lady had no doubt been working on, and over two small family photos of young boys, one in a college gown and the other in red jacket. like a soldier. When she fell asleep, Rebecca chose this one to dream of.

At four o'clock on a summer morning so rosy that it even made Great Gaunt Street merry, the faithful Tinker, having woken up his bedmate and told him to prepare for departure, unlocked and unlocked the door to the great hall overheard the sleepy echoes in the street), and, heading towards Oxford Street, summoned a coach from a booth there. It is unnecessary to state the vehicle number, or to state that the driver was parked so early in the Swallow Street area, in the hope that a young male, returning from the tavern, might need help from his vehicle, and pay for it with the generosity of drunkenness.

It is also needless to say that the driver, if he had any hopes such as those stated above, was grossly disappointed; and that the worthy baronet whom he led to the city did not give him a single centime more than his fare. It was in vain that Jehu appealed and stormed; that he threw Miss Sharp's music boxes into the gutter of the 'Necks, and swore he would obey the law of his tariff.

"You better not," said one of the ostlers; "this is Sir Pitt Crawley."

"It is so, Joe," cried the baronet approvingly; "and I would like to see the man can do me."

"So should oi," Joe said, grimacing sullenly, and mounting the baronet's baggage onto the roof of the coach.

" Keep the box for me, chief, " cried the deputy to the coachman ; who replied, " Yes, Sir Pitt ", with a hat-trick and rage in his soul (for he had promised the box to a young man in Cambridge, who would have given a crown to a certainty), and Miss Sharp was accommodated with a rear seat inside the car, which could be said to transport it to the wide world.

How the young man from Cambridge sulked put his five coats in front; but he did reconcile when little Miss Sharp was forced to leave the car and get in next to him - when he covered her up with one of his Benjamins and became perfectly in good spirits - how the gentleman asthmatic, the lady primi her sacred honor, she had never traveled in a public car before (there is always such a lady in a coach, alas! was; for the coaches, where are they?), and the fat widow with the bottle of brandy, took their place inside - how the porter asked them all for money, and got six pence from the gentleman and five greasy pence from the fat widow - and how the car finally pulled away - now threading through the dark alleys of Aldersgate, then slamming through the blue dome of St. Paul's, quickly jingling through the strangers entrance to Fleet-Market, which, along with Exeter 'Change, is now gone to the shadow world - how they passed the polar bear in Piccadilly, and saw the the dew rising from the market - the gardens of Knightsbridge - how Turnhamgreen, Brentwood, Bagshot, were adopted, need not be said here. But the author of these pages, who once continued and at the same time radiant, the same remarkable journey, can only think of it with sweet and tender regret. Where is the road now, and its happy incidents in life? Isn't there a Chelsea or Greenwich for the honest, button- nosed old coachmen ? I wonder where are these good people? Is old Weller alive or dead? and the waiters, yes, and the inns they were waiting in, and the cold rounds of beef inside, and the stunted ostler, with his blue nose and clinking bucket, where is he, and where is his generation ? To those great geniuses now in petticoats, who will write novels for the children of the beloved reader, these men and things will be as much legend and history as Nineveh, or Lionheart , or Jack Sheppard. For them, the stagecoaches will have become romances, a team of four spans as fabulous as Bucephalus or Black Bess. Ah, as their coats shone, as the stable men took off their clothes and walked away, ah, as their tails trembled, as with the smoldering sides at the back of the stage, they wisely went into the yard of the hostel. Alas! we will never hear the horn sing at midnight again, nor will we see the stakes open. But where does the four- seater Trafalgar light coach take us ? Let's land at Queen's Crawley without further rambling, and see how fast Miss Rebecca Sharp gets there.

CHAPTER VIII

Private and confidential

Miss Rebecca Sharp to Miss Amelia Sedley, Russell Square, London. (Free.— Pitt Crawley.)

MY VERY DEAR, VERY SWEET AMELIA,

With what a mixture of joy and sorrow I take up my pen to write to my dearest friend ! Oh, what a change between today and yesterday! Now I am friendless and alone; yesterday I was at home, in the sweet company of a sister whom I will always cherish!

I will not tell you in what tears and in what sadness I spent the fatal night when I separated from you. YOU went on Tuesday in joy and happiness, with your mother and YOUR DEDICATED YOUNG SOLDIER by your side; and I've been thinking about you all night, dancing at the Perkins', the prettiest, I'm sure, of all the ladies at the ball. I was brought by the groom in the old car to Sir Pitt Crawley's town house , where after John the groom behaved in the most rude and insolent manner with me (alas! It was sure to be 'insult poverty and misfortune!), I was delivered to the care of Sir P., and made to spend the night in an old dark bed, and next to a horrible dark old housekeeper, who keeps the House. I haven't slept in a single blink of an eye all night.

Sir Pitt is not what we silly girls imagined when reading Cecilia in Chiswick that a baronet must be. Nothing, indeed, less like Lord Orville can be imagined. Imagine a stocky old man, short, vulgar and very dirty, dressed in old clothes and shabby old gaiters, who smokes a horrible pipe and cooks his horrible supper in a saucepan. He speaks with a country accent, and insults a lot at the old maid, the cab driver who took us to the inn from which the carriage left, and on which I made the trip OUTSIDE FOR THE MOST PART OF THE ROAD.

I was awakened at daybreak by the maid, and having arrived at the inn, I was first placed in the coach. But, when we got to a place called Leakington, where the rain started to fall really hard - would you believe it ? - I was forced to go out; as Sir Pitt owns the car, and as a passenger came to Mudbury, who wanted an indoor place, I was forced to go out into the rain, where, however, a young man from Cambridge College very kindly told me sheltered in one of its several large coats.

This gentleman and the guard seemed to know Sir Pitt very well and laughed at him a lot. They both agreed to call him an old jerk; which means a very stingy and stingy person. He never gives anyone money, they said (and that meanness I hate); and the young gentleman pointed out to me that we drove very slowly for the last two legs of the road, because Sir Pitt was on the stall, and because he owns the horses for this part of the journey. " But won't I whip them in Squashmore, when I take the ribbons ?" " Said the young Cantab. "And keep them well, Master Jack," the guard said. When I understood the meaning of that phrase, and Master Jack intended to lead the rest of the way and take revenge on Sir Pitt's horses, of course, I laughed too.

A splendid carriage and four horses, however, covered with coats of arms, awaited us at Mudbury, four miles from Queen's Crawley, and we entered the baronet's park in good condition. There is a lovely mile-long avenue leading up to the house, and the woman at the door of the lodge (on whose pillars is a serpent and a dove, the followers of Crawley's·arms), gave us a certain many curtsies as she opened the old carved iron gates, which resemble those of the odious Chiswick.

" There is an avenue," said Sir Pitt, "a mile long. There are six thousand pounds of wood in these trees. Do you call it nothing? He said avenue — EVENUE, and nothing — NOTHHINK, so funny; and he had a Mr. Hodson, his Mudbury doe, in the carriage with him, and they talked about foreclosure, and selling, and dewatering and subsoiling, and a lot of tenants and farming - a lot more that I couldn't understand. Sam Miles had been caught poaching, and Peter Bailey had finally gone home from work. " Serve it well, " said Sir Pitt ; "He and his family have cheated on me on this farm for 150 years." An old tenant, I guess, who couldn't pay his rent. Sir Pitt could have said "him and his family", of course; but rich baronets do not need to worry about grammar, as poor governesses should be.

As I passed, I noticed a beautiful church steeple rising above some old elms in the park; and in front of them, in the middle of a lawn and a few outbuildings, an old red house with tall ivy-covered chimneys, and windows shining in the sun. "Is this your church, sir? I said.

"Yes, hang it up," (said Sir Pitt, only he used, my dear, A MUCH MORE WICKEDER WORD); "How 's Buty, Hodson?" Buty is my brother Bute, my dear, my brother the pastor. Buty and the Beast, I call him, ha ha!

Hodson laughed too, then, sounding more serious and nodding, said , 'I'm afraid he's better, Sir Pitt. He was on his pony yesterday, looking at our corn.

"Taking care of his tithes, hanged (only he used the same word wicked). Will brandy and brandy never kill him? He's as tough as old Whatecallum - old Methusalem. "

Mr. Hodson laughed again. "The young men came home from college. They beat John Scroggins until he was almost dead."

" Whop my second keeper !" " Bellowed Sir Pitt.

"It was on the parish's land, sir," replied Mr. Hodson; and Sir Pitt, enraged, swore that if he caught them poaching on his soil, he would transport them, by the lord, he would. However, he said, "I sold the live presentation , Hodson; none of this race will get it, I war'nt " ; and Mr. Hodson said he was absolutely right: and I have no doubt that the two brothers disagree, as brothers often are, and sisters too. Don't you remember the two Miss Scratchleys in Chiswick, how they always fought and argued and Mary Box, how she always hit Louisa?

Soon seeing two little boys picking up sticks in the wood, Mr. Hodson jumped out of the car, at Sir Pitt's order, and rushed at them with his whip. "Throw yourself into them, Hodson," exclaimed the baronet; " Family their little souls and bring them home, the vagabonds ; I will commit them as sure as my name is Pitt. " Soon we heard the whip Hodson slam on the shoulders of the poor wretched little whiny, and Sir Pitt, seeing that the perpetrators were in custody, walked to the room.

All the servants were ready to meet us, and. . .

Here, my dear, I was interrupted last night by a terrible knock on my door: and who do you think it was? Sir Pitt Crawley in his nightcap and dressing gown, such a figure! As I backed away from such a visitor, he stepped forward and grabbed my candle. "No candles after eleven o'clock, Miss Becky," he said. "Go to bed in the dark, pretty little rascal" (that's what he called me), "and unless you want me to come and get the candle every night, be careful and be in bed. eleven o'clock. And with that, he and Mr. Horrocks the butler both laughed. Rest assured that I will no longer encourage their visits. They released two huge sleuths at night, which all night long were screaming and howling at the moon. "I call the dog Gorer," said Sir Pitt; "He killed a man that this dog has, and is the master of a bull, and the mother that I called Flora; but now I call her Aroarer, because she's too old to bite. Haw, haw!

In front of Queen's Crawley House, which is an obnoxious old-fashioned red brick mansion, with tall chimneys and Queen Bess style gables, there is a terrace flanked by the family's dove and serpent, and on which the large hall door opens. And oh, my dear, the great hall, I'm sure, is as big and as dark as the great hall of dear Udolpho Castle. It has a big fireplace, in which we could put half of Miss Pinkerton's school, and the grill is big enough to roast at least one ox. Around the room hang I don't know how many generations of Crawleys, some with beards and strawberries, some with huge wigs and toes turned out, some in long straight corsets and dresses that look too steep as turns, and some with long loops, and oh, my dear! almost no remainder at all. At the end of the corridor, the large staircase all in black oak, as dismal as it is, and on either side are high doors surmounted by stag heads, leading to the billiard room and the library, and to the large living room yellow. and the rooms in the morning. I think there are at least twenty rooms on the first floor; one of them has the bed in which Queen Elizabeth slept; and I was led by my new students through all these beautiful apartments this morning. We don't make them any less gloomy, I promise you, by always having the shutters closed ; and there is barely one of the apartments, but when the light was introduced, I expected to see a ghost in the room. We have a classroom on the second floor, with my bedroom on one side and the ladies' bedroom on the other. Then there are the apartments of Mr. Pitt — M. Crawley, he's called - the eldest son, and Chambers of Mr. Rawdon Crawley - he's an officer like SOMEBODY, and gone with his regiment. There is no shortage of space, I assure you. You could put all the folks in Russell Square in the house, I think, and have some space to spare.

Half an hour after our arrival, the big dinner bell rang, and I went downstairs with my two students (they are very thin, insignificant little bits of ten and eight years old). I came down in your dear muslin dress (about which that obnoxious Mrs. Pinner was so rude, because you gave it to me); because I should be treated like a member of the family, except on company days, when the ladies and I have to dine upstairs.

Well, the big dinner bell rang, and we all gathered in the parlor where my Lady Crawley is sitting. She is the second Lady Crawley and the mother of the young girls. She was the daughter of a hardware store and her marriage was considered a perfect marriage. She looks like she was beautiful once, and her eyes still cry for the loss of her beauty. She is pale and skinny with tall shoulders, and obviously doesn't have a say for herself. Her stepson, Mr. Crawley, was also in the room. He was in full dress, pompous as an undertaker. He is pale, thin, ugly, silent; he has slender legs, no breasts, hay sideburns, and straw-colored hair. There is the very image of his holy mother on the mantelpiece: Griselda from the noble house of Binkie.

"This is the new housekeeper, Mr. Crawley," said Lady Crawley, stepping forward and taking my hand. "Miss Sharp."

"O! " " Said Mr. Crawley, and nudged his head forward once and again began to read a large pamphlet he was busy with.

"I hope you will be nice to my daughters," said Lady Crawley, with her pink eyes still filled with tears.

"The law, mom, of course she will," said the elder: and I saw at a glance that I don't need to be afraid of THIS woman. "My lady is served," said the butler in black, in a huge white ruffled shirt, which appeared to have been one of Queen Elizabeth's strawberries pictured in the hall; and so, taking Mr. Crawley's arm, she led the way to the dining-room, where I followed with my little pupils in each hand.

Sir Pitt was already in the room with a silver jug. He had just gone to the cellar and was also in full dress; that is to say, he had taken off his gaiters and was showing his little stocky legs in black woolen stockings. The sideboard was covered with an old shiny plate - old cups, both gold and silver; old trays and cruets, like the Rundell and Bridge store. Everything on the table was also silver, and two footmen, with red hair and canary liveries, stood on either side of the sideboard.

Mr. Crawley said a long grace, and Sir Pitt said amen, and the big silver plate covers have been removed.

"What do we have for dinner, Betsy?" said the baronet.

"Mutton broth, I believe, Sir Pitt," replied Lady Crawley.

"Mutton with turnips," added the butler gravely (pronounce, please, moutongonavvy); "and the soup is a Scottish mutton soup. The sides contain potatoes in brine and cauliflower in water."

" Mutton de mutton," said the baronet, "and a good devilish thing. What BOAT was it, Horrocks, and when did you kill? "One of the black-faced Scots, Sir Pitt: we killed Thursday.

" Who took it ? "

"Steel , of Mudbury, has taken the saddle and both legs, Sir Pitt; but he said the last one was too young and confused, Sir Pitt.

"Would you like some soup, miss ah… miss Blunt?" Mr Crawley said.

" Scottish capital broth, my dear," said Sir Pitt, "although they call it by a French name.

"I believe it is the custom, sir, in decent society," said Mr. Crawley, haughtily, "to call the dish as I have called it"; and it was served to us on deep silver plates by the footmen in canary coats, with the mutton with turnips. Then we brought "beer and water" and served young girls in wine glasses. I am not a beer judge, but I can safely say that I prefer water.

While we were having our meal, Sir Pitt took the opportunity to ask what had become of the sheep's shoulders.

"I believe they were eaten in the servants' room," said my lady humbly.

" They were, my lady, " Horrocks said, " and we won't get there either.

Sir Pitt laughed like a horse and continued his conversation with Mr. Horrocks. "This little black pig of the Kent sow breed must be a rare fat now."

"It's not quite flashy, Sir Pitt," said the butler with the most serious air, at which Sir Pitt, and with him the ladies this time, laughed violently.

" Miss Crawley, Miss Rose Crawley, " said Mr. Crawley, " your laughter seems extremely inappropriate to me. "

'It doesn't matter, my lord,' said the baronet, 'we'll try the pig on Saturday. Kill John Horrocks on a Saturday morning. Miss Sharp loves pork, doesn't she, Miss Sharp?

And I think that's the whole conversation I remember at dinner. When the meal was over, a jug of hot water was placed in front of Sir Pitt, along with a bottle containing, I believe, rum. Mr. Horrocks served me and my students three small glasses of wine, and a bumper was poured for my lady. When we retired, she pulled out a huge, endless piece of knitting from her work drawer ; the young ladies began to play cribbage with a dirty deck of cards. We only had one candle lit, but it was in a beautiful old silver candlestick, and after a few questions from my lady, I had the choice of having fun between a volume of sermons and a pamphlet on Corn Laws, which Mr. Crawley had read before dinner.

So we sat for an hour until footsteps were heard.

- Put away the cards, girls, cried my lady in a great trembling; " Put down Mr. Crawley's books , Miss Sharp " ; and these orders had hardly been obeyed, when Mr. Crawley entered the room.

'We will resume yesterday's speech, gentlemen,' he said, 'and you will each read a page in turn, so that Mademoiselle a ... Mademoiselle Short has the opportunity to hear you; and the poor girls began to spell a long dismal sermon delivered in Bethesda Chapel, Liverpool, in the name of the mission for the Chickasaw Indians. Wasn't it a lovely evening ?

At ten o'clock the servants were ordered to call Sir Pitt and the household to prayer. Sir Pitt arrived first, very flushed and rather unsteady in his walk; and after him the butler, the canaries, Mr. Crawley's man, three other men, very smelling of the stable, and four women, one of whom, I noticed, was very dressed, and who threw me a look of great contempt. as she fell to her knees.

After Mr. Crawley had finished haranguing and exhibiting, we received our candles, then went to bed; and then I was disturbed in my writing, as I described it to my very dear and very sweet Amélie.

Good night. A thousand, a thousand, a thousand kisses!

Saturday. - This morning, at five o'clock, I heard the cry of the little black pig. Rose and Violet introduced him to me yesterday; and to the stables, and to the kennel, and to the gardener, who gathered fruit to send to the market, and to whom they begged harshly for a bunch of greenhouse grapes; but he said Sir Pitt had numbered every "Man Jack" of them, and that would be as much as his place was worth giving. The darling girls grabbed a foal in a paddock and asked if I wanted to ride, and started to ride themselves, when the groom, coming up with horrible curses, chased them away.

Lady Crawley is still knitting the combed. Sir Pitt is still drunk every night; and, I believe, sits with Horrocks, the butler. Mr. Crawley always reads sermons in the evenings, and in the mornings is locked in his office, or goes to Mudbury, on county business, or to Squashmore, where he preaches, Wednesdays and Fridays, to the tenants there. .

One hundred thousand grateful loves to your dear mom and dad. Has your poor brother recovered from his racketeering? Oh dear! Oh dear! How men should beware of the wrong punch!

Always and always yours REBECCA

All in all, I think it's just as good for our dear Amelia Sedley in Russell Square that she and Miss Sharp are going their separate ways. Rebecca is a funny and funny creature, of course; and these descriptions of the poor lady mourning the loss of her beauty, and of the gentleman "with straw-colored sideburns and straw-colored hair", are undoubtedly very intelligent and show great knowledge of the world. That she could have, on her knees, thought of something better than the Miss Horrocks ribbons, perhaps struck us both. But my kind reader will be happy to remember that this story is titled "Vanity Fair" and that Vanity Fair is a very vain, mean, foolish place, full of all kinds of hoaxes, falsehoods and pretensions. And while the moralist, who stands forward on the cover (a faithful portrait of your humble servant), claims to wear neither robe nor band, but only the same long-eared livery in which his congregation is clad: yet look- you, one is bound to speak the truth as far as one knows it, whether one is wearing a cap and bells or a shovel hat; and an unpleasant affair must come out during such an enterprise.

I heard a brother from the storytelling profession, in Naples, preach to a pack of good-for-nothing lazy honesty by the sea, get into such rage and such passion with some of the wicked including the wicked acts that he described and invented, which the public could not resist; and they and the poet would burst together in a roar of curses and executions against the fictional monster of the tale, so that the hat turned, and the bajocchi fell into it, in the midst of a perfect storm of sympathy.

In the small theaters of Paris, on the other hand, you will not only hear the people shouting "Ah rascal! Ah monster! And curse the tyrant of the lodges room; but the actors themselves positively refuse to play the wicked roles, such as those of the infamous Englishmen, brutal Cossacks, etc., and prefer to appear at a lower salary, in their true characters of loyal French. I oppose the two stories to each other, so that you can see clearly that it is not for simple mercenary motives that the current actor wants to show himself and beat his scoundrels; but because he has a sincere hatred of it, which he cannot contain, and which must find an outlet in the appropriate abuse and bad language.

I then warn my "kyind friends" that I am going to tell a heart-wrenching wickedness and complicated crime story - but, I trust, intensely interesting -. My rascals are not rascals with milk and water, I promise you. When we get to the right places, we won't spare the beautiful language - No, no! But when we roam the quiet country, we must necessarily be calm. A storm in a settling pond is nonsense. We'll save that sort of thing for the mighty ocean and the lonely midnight. This chapter is very sweet. Others — But we're not anticipating CES.

And as we move our characters forward, I'll ask permission, as a man and a brother, not only to introduce them, but sometimes to come down from the platform and talk about them: if they are. good and benevolent, loving them and shaking hands with them: if they are fools, making fun of them confidentially in the reader's sleeve; if they are mean and heartless, abuse them in the strongest terms politeness admits.

If not, you might think it was I who sneered at the practice of devotion, which Miss Sharp finds so ridiculous; that it was I who laughed with good humor at the tottering old Silenus of a baronet, while the laughter comes from someone who has respect only for prosperity, and who has eyes only for Success. Such people there live and thrive in the world - without faith, without hope, without charity: let us have to them, dear friends, with strength and strength. There are some, and very successful too, simple charlatans and imbeciles : and it is to fight and expose such as these, no doubt, that the laughter is made.

CHAPTER IX

Family portraits

Sir Pitt Crawley was a philosopher with a taste for what is called low life. His first marriage to the daughter of the noble Binkie had been made under the auspices of his parents; and as he often told Lady Crawley during her lifetime, she was such a quarrelsome high-bred Jade that when she died he was hanged if he ever took another of his kind, at the Madam's death he kept his promise and was selected for a second wife Miss Rose Dawson, daughter of Mr. John Thomas Dawson, hardware store, of Mudbury. What a happy woman Rose was to be my Lady Crawley!

Let us pose the elements of his happiness. First, she abandoned Peter Butt, a young man who kept her company, and, as a result of her disappointment in love, began to smuggle, poach and do a thousand other bad things. Then she quarreled, as in duty, with all the friends and close friends of her youth, who, of course, could not be received by my Lady at Queen's Crawley, and neither did she find it in her new rank and his new abode of people who wanted to accommodate him. Who ever did? Sir Huddleston Fuddleston had three daughters who all hoped to be Lady Crawley. Sir Giles Wapshot's family were insulted that one of Wapshot's daughters had no preference in marriage, and the remaining county baronets were outraged at their comrade's misalliance. No matter the commoners, whom we will let bitch anonymously.

Sir Pitt didn't care, as he put it, of a brazen farden for either of them. He had his pretty Rose, and what more could a man need than to indulge himself? So he got drunk every night: sometimes beating his pretty Rose: leaving her in Hampshire when he went to London for the parliamentary session, without a single friend in the world. Even Mrs Bute Crawley, the rector's wife, refused to visit him because she said she would never give precedence to a tradesman's daughter.

How the only endowments with which nature had endowed Lady Crawley were those of rosy cheeks and white skin, and how she had no kind of character, no talents, no opinions, no occupations, no amusements, no such vigorous vigor. he soul and fierceness of character which often falls to the fate of entirely stupid women, her hold on Sir Pitt's affections was not very great. Her roses faded from her cheeks, and the pretty freshness left her figure after the birth of a few children, and she has become a simple machine in her husband's house which has no more use than the piano to tail of the late Lady

Crawley. Being a fair-skinned woman, she wore light-colored clothing, as most blondes do, and preferably appeared in streaked sea green or dull sky blue. She worked this combed day and night, or other pieces of the same kind. She has had blankets on all of Crawley's beds in a few years. She had a small flower garden, for which she was rather fond of; but beyond that no other likes or dislikes. When her husband was rude to her, she was listless: every time he hit her, she cried. She didn't have enough character to start drinking, and moaned all day, slipped and curled. O Vanity Fair — Vanity Fair! It could have been, without you, a cheerful young girl - Peter Butt and Rose a happy man and woman, on a comfortable farm, with a warm family; and an honest portion of pleasures, worries, hopes and struggles, but a title, a coach and four are more valuable toys than happiness at Vanity Fair: what if Harry the Eighth or Bluebeard were alive now and wanted a tenth wife, are you guessing he couldn't get the prettiest girl to be featured this season?

The languid boredom of their mother did not arouse, as one can suppose, much affection in her little girls, but they were very happy in the room of the servants and in the stables; and the Scottish gardener fortunately having a good wife and a few good children, they had some healthy society and education in his lodge, which was the only education afforded them until the arrival of Miss Sharp.

Her engagement was due to the remonstrances of Mr. Pitt Crawley, the only friend or protector Lady Crawley had ever had, and the only person, besides her children, for whom she had a weak attachment. Mr. Pitt took after the noble Binkies, from whom he descended, and was a very polite and decent gentleman. When he became a man and returned from Christchurch, he began to reform the loose discipline of the hall, despite his father fearful of him. He was a man of such rigid refinement that he would have preferred to starve than to have dined without a white tie. Once, when he was just out of college, and when Horrocks the butler brought him a letter without first placing it on a tray, he glanced at this servant and gave him such a sharp speech, that Horrocks shuddered. always in front of him; the whole household bowed to him: Lady Crawley's curly papers came off earlier when he was home: Sir Pitt's muddy gaiters are gone; and if this incorrigible old man still stuck to other old habits, he never bothered with rum and water in the presence of his son, and spoke to his servants only in a very reserved and polite manner. ; and these people noticed that Sir Pitt never cursed Lady Crawley while his son was in the room.

It was he who taught the butler to say: "My lady is served," and who insisted on delivering Madame to dinner. He rarely spoke to her, but when he did, it was with the utmost respect; and he never let her leave the apartment without getting up in the most majestic manner to open the door, and make an elegant greeting as she left.

In Eton his name was Miss Crawley; and there, I'm sorry to say it, his younger brother Rawdon was licking him violently. But although his roles were not brilliant, he made up for his lack of talent with a meritorious industry, and was never known, for eight years in school, to be subjected to that punishment which is generally believed to be only a cherub can escape.

In college, his career was of course very honorable. And there he prepared for public life, into which he was to be introduced by the patronage of his grandfather, Lord Binkie, studying ancient and modern orators with great assiduity, and speaking incessantly in societies of debate. But although he had a beautiful flow of words, and delivered his little voice with great pomp and pleasure, and he never put forward any feeling or opinion that was not perfectly trite and outdated, and backed by a Latin quote ; yet he failed in one way or another, despite a mediocrity that should have ensured success for any man. He didn't even get the prize poem, which all of his friends said he was sure about.

After leaving college, he became Lord Binkie's private secretary, then was appointed attaché to the legation at Pumpernickel, a post he filled with perfect honor, and brought dispatches composed of Strasbourg pie to the Minister of Foreign Affairs of the day. . After remaining ten years attached (several years after the late Lord Binkie's demise) and finding advancement slow, he finally gave up diplomatic service with some disgust and began to become a country gentleman.

He wrote a pamphlet on Malt on his return to England (for he was an ambitious man, and always liked to be in front of the public), and took an important part in the question of black emancipation. Then he became friends with Mr. Wilberforce, whose policies he admired, and had this famous correspondence with the Reverend Silas Hornblower, on the Ashantee mission. He was in London, if not for the parliamentary session, at least in May, for religious meetings. In the countryside, he was a magistrate, visitor and active lecturer among those who had not received religious instruction. He was said to pay his addresses to Lady Jane Sheepshanks, Lord Southdown's third daughter, and whose sister, Lady Emily, wrote these sweet tracts, "The Sailor's True Binnacle" and "The Applewoman of Finchley Common".

Miss Sharp's accounts of her job at Queen's Crawley were not caricatures. There he subjected the servants to the devotional exercises mentioned above, in which (and so much the better) he made his father participate. He sponsored an independent meeting house in the parish of Crawley, much to the indignation of his uncle the rector, and to the great joy of Sir Pitt, who was brought in himself once or twice, which occasioned violent sermons at Crawley Parish Church, conducted point blank on the baronet's old Gothic bench. Honest Sir Pitt, however, did not feel the force of these speeches, for he always took his nap during the sermon.

Mr. Crawley was very serious, for the good of the nation and of the Christian world, that the old gentleman yield to him his place in Parliament; but this the elder constantly refused to do. Both were of course too cautious to give up the fifteen cents a year that the second seat brought (at that time occupied by Mr. Quadroon, with carte blanche on the question of the Slaves); indeed, the family estate was in great embarrassment, and the income from the borough was of great use to the house of Queen's Crawley.

He had never recovered the heavy fine imposed on Walpole Crawley, Chief Baronet, for concussions at the Office of the tape and sealing wax. Sir Walpole was a cheerful boy, eager to grab and spend money (Alieni appetens, sui profusus, as Mr. Crawley would point out with a sigh), and in his day loved across the county for constant drunkenness and the hospitality that was maintained. at Queen's Crawley. The cellars were then full of burgundy, the kennels of hounds, and the stables of valiant hunters; now the horses Queen's Crawley owned were going to plow or run in the Trafalgar Coach; and it was with a team of these same horses, on a day off, that Miss Sharp was brought to the hall; for the boorish man he was, Sir Pitt was concerned with his dignity when he was at home, and rarely hunted with only four horses, and although he dined on boiled mutton, he always had three servants for him. to serve.

If mere parsimony could have made a man rich, Sir Pitt Crawley could have become very rich - if he had been a lawyer in a country town, with no capital but his brain, it is very possible that he would have profited from it. , and could have acquired for himself a very considerable influence and competence. But unfortunately he was blessed with a good reputation and a vast though crowded estate, both of which were more likely to hurt him than advance him. He had a taste for law, which cost him several thousand a year; and being far too smart to be robbed, as he said, by a single agent, let his affairs be mismanaged by a dozen, of whom he was all equally suspicious. He was such a shrewd landlord that he found hardly anything but bankrupt tenants ; and a farmer so close that he almost wanted the seed in the earth, whereupon vengeful nature resented him for the harvests which she granted to more liberal cultivators. He was speculating in every way he could ; he worked in the mines; bought channel shares; coaches; took government contracts, and was the busiest man and magistrate in his county. As he did not want to pay honest agents in his granite quarry, he had the satisfaction of finding that four overseers fled and took fortunes with them to America. For want of proper precautions, his coal mines filled with water: the government threw his rotten beef contract over his hands; and for his carriage horses, every postal owner in the kingdom knew he was losing more horses than any man in the kingdom. country , undernourishment and cheap shopping. By character, he was sociable and far from being proud; he rather preferred the company of a farmer or a horse dealer to that of a gentleman, like Monsignor, his son: he liked to drink, to swear, to joke with the daughters of the farmers: he was never known to give a shilling or do a good deed, but was in a joking, sly and laughing mood, and cut his joke and drank his glass with a tenant and sold it the next day; or else laugh with the poacher he was carrying with the same good humor. His politeness for the fair sex has already been mentioned by Miss Rebecca Sharp - in short, the whole baronnetage, peerage, community of England did not contain a more cunning, mean, selfish, stupid and disreputable old man. That blood-red hand of Sir Pitt Crawley would be in anyone's pocket except his own; and it is with sorrow and sorrow that as admirers of the British aristocracy we find ourselves compelled to admit the existence of so many bad qualities in a person whose name is in Debrett.

A big reason Mr. Crawley had such a hold over his father's affections was the result of financial arrangements. The baronet owed his son a sum of money on his mother's joint, which he did not consider convenient to pay; indeed, he had an almost invincible reluctance to pay anyone, and could only be made to pay off his debts by force. Miss Sharp calculated (for she became, as we will quickly learn, enthroned in most family secrets) that the mere payment of her creditors was costing the honorable baronet several hundred a year; but it was a delight he could not give up; he had a savage pleasure in keeping the unfortunate waiting, and in shifting the time of satisfaction from court to court and from quarter to quarter. What good is it to be in Parliament, he said, if you have to pay your debts? Thus, in fact, his position as a senator was of great use to him.

Fair Vanity-Fair vanity ! He was a man who did not know how to spell and who did not care to read, who had the habits and cunning of a boor: whose purpose in life was to joke: who had never had a taste, of emotion or pleasure, sordid and filthy; and yet he had rank, and honors, and power, one way or another: and was a dignitary of the country, and a pillar of the state. He was a grand sheriff and rode in a golden coach. Great ministers and statesmen courted him; and in Vanity Fair he had a higher place than the brightest genius or spotless virtue.

Sir Pitt had an unmarried half-sister who inherited her mother's great fortune, and although the Baronet offered to borrow this money from her on a mortgage, Miss Crawley declined the offer and preferred the security of the funds. She had, however, signaled her intention to leave her inheritance between Sir Pitt's second son and the parsonage family, and had paid Rawdon Crawley's debts once or twice in his college and military career. Miss Crawley was, therefore, an object of great respect when she came to Queen's Crawley, for she had a scale with her banker that would have made her beloved anywhere.

What dignity it gives to an old lady, this scale at the banker! With what tenderness we look at her faults if she is a relative (and each reader has twenty), what a good old creature we find her! How Hobbs and Dobbs' junior partner drives her smiling towards the car with the diamond on it, and the fat coachman hissing! How, when she comes to visit us, we usually find the opportunity to let our friends know about her position in the world! We say (and with perfect truth) that I would have liked to have had Miss MacWhirter's signature on a check for 5,000 pounds. She wouldn't miss it, your wife said. She's my aunt, you say, in an easy and careless way, when your friend asks if Miss MacWhirter is a relative. Your wife never ceases to send her little expressions of affection, your little girls work for her on worsted baskets, cushions and footrests. What a warm fire there is in her room when she comes to visit you, although your wife does not lace her ! The house during his stay takes on a festive, neat, warm, jovial, cozy aspect that is not visible in other seasons. You yourself, dear sir, forget to go to bed after dinner, and all of a sudden (though you invariably get lost) very fond of a rubber. What good dinners you have - daily game, Malmsey-Madeira, and endless London fish. Even the servants of the kitchen participate in the general prosperity ; and somehow during the stay of Miss MacWhirter's fat coachman the beer got much stronger, and the consumption of tea and sugar in the nursery (where her maid takes her meals) is not considered at all. Is this the case, or is it not? I appeal to the middle classes. Ah, gracious powers ! I would like you to send me an old aunt - a young aunt - an aunt with a diamond on her car, and a front of light coffee colored hair - how my kids should work bags for her, and my Julia and I would make him feel comfortable! Sweet — sweet sight ! Idiot — crazy dream !

CHAPTER X

Miss Sharp is starting to make friends

And now, being received as a member of the amiable family whose portraits we have sketched in the previous pages, it naturally became Rebecca's duty to surrender, as she said, pleasing to her benefactors, and to gain their trust in the maximum of it. Power. Who can only admire this quality of gratitude in an orphan without protection ; and, if a little selfishness entered into his calculations, who can say that his prudence was perfectly justifiable? "I am alone in the world," said the friendless girl. " I have nothing to look for other than what my own work can do for me ; and while that pink-faced little Amelia, who doesn't have half of my senses, has ten thousand pounds and a secure establishment, poor Rebecca (and my figure is much better than hers) has no confidence but 'in herself and in her own mind. Well, let's see if my mind can't provide me with an honorable interview, and if one day or another I can't show Miss Amelia my real superiority over her. I don't like poor Amelia: who can hate such a harmless and good-natured creature? Only it will be a beautiful day when I can take my place above her in the world, for why, indeed, should I not? This is how our romantic girlfriend had visions of the future - one should not be scandalized either that, in all her castles in the air, a husband was the main inhabitant. What else can young women think of if not husbands? What else are their dear mothers thinking about ? "I must be my own mom," said Rebecca; not without a tingling feeling of defeat, thinking back to his little mishap with Jos Sedley.

So she wisely decided to make her position within the Queen's Crawley family comfortable and secure, and to that end resolved to make friends around her who might interfere with her comfort.

As my Lady Crawley was not one of those characters, and a woman for that matter so indolent and characterless that she had no importance in her own household, Rebecca soon found that he was not. not at all necessary to cultivate common sense. will - indeed, impossible to get it. She spoke to her pupils about their "poor mother"; and although she treated this lady with every show of cold respect, it was to the rest of the family that she wisely directed the main part of her attentions.

With the young people, for whom she was fully applauded, her method was quite simple. She did not bother their young brains with too much learning, but, on the contrary, let them do their own thing when it comes to education; for which instruction is more effective than self-instruction? The elder was rather fond of books, and as there was in the old Queen's Crawley library a considerable supply of light literature from the last century, both in French and in English (they had been purchased by the secretary of the Band and Office of Sealing Wax at the time of her disgrace), and as no one has ever bothered the shelves except herself, Rebecca has been pleasantly allowed and, so to speak, playing, to give Miss Rose Crawley lots of instructions.

She and Mlle Rose have thus read together many delicious French and English works, among which we can cite those of the learned Dr. Smollett, the ingenious Mr. Henry Fielding, the gracious and fantastic Mr. Crébillon the younger, whom our immortal poet Gray so admired, and of the universal Monsieur de Voltaire. Once, when Mr. Crawley asked what the young people were reading, the housekeeper replied " Smollett ". " Oh , Smollett, " Mr. Crawley said, quite satisfied. "His story is more boring, but by no means as dangerous as that of Mr. Hume." Is that history you're reading? "Yes," said Miss Rose; without adding, however, that it was the story of Mr. Humphrey Clinker. Another time he was quite scandalized to find his sister with a book of French plays ; but as the housekeeper noticed that it was to acquire the French idiom in conversation, he wanted to be satisfied with it. Mr. Crawley, as a diplomat, was extremely proud of his own ability to speak the French language (for he was still a world of people), and quite pleased with the compliments the housekeeper continually paid him for his competence.

Miss Violet's tastes were, on the contrary, coarser and noisier than her sister's. She knew the sequestered places where the hens laid their eggs. She could climb a tree to strip the nests of the feathered singers of their spotted loot. And his pleasure was to ride the young foals and to roam the plains like Camille. She was the favorite of her father and of the stable men. She was the darling, and with the terror of the cook; for she discovered the dens of the jars of jam, and attacked them when they were within her reach. She and her sister were engaged in constant battles. None of these peccadilloes, if Miss Sharp found them, she did not tell Lady Crawley; who would have told them to the father, or worse, to Mr. Crawley; but promised not to say if Miss Violet would be a good girl and would love her housekeeper.

With Mr. Crawley, Miss Sharp was respectful and obedient. She consulted him on passages in French which she did not understand, although his mother was French, and which he interpreted to his satisfaction: and, in addition to having helped him in secular literature, he was kind enough to choose books for her. of a more serious tendency, and address much of his conversation to him. She admired, beyond measure, his speech at the Quashimaboo-Aid Society; was interested in his pamphlet on malt: was often affected, to tears, by his one-night stands, and said: "Oh, thank you, sir", with a sigh and a look to the sky, it was sometimes he deigns to shake his hand. " Blood is everything, after all," this aristocratic cleric would say. "How Miss Sharp is awakened by my words, when no one here is touched." I am too good for them, too delicate. I have to familiarize myself with my style, but she understands it. His mother was a Montmorency.

Indeed, it was from this famous family, it seems, that Miss Sharp, on her mother's side, descended. Of course, she didn't say her mother had taken the stage; that would have shocked Mr. Crawley's religious scruples. How many noble emigrants had this horrible revolution plunged into misery! She had several stories about her ancestors before she was several months in the house; some which Mr. Crawley happened to find in D'Hozier's dictionary, which was in the library, and which reinforced his belief in their truth, and in the high race of Rebecca. Should we assume from this curiosity and digging through dictionaries, could our heroine assume that Mr. Crawley was interested in her? No, only in a friendly manner. Didn't we say he was attached to Lady Jane Sheepshanks?

He once or twice berated Rebecca on the advisability of playing backgammon with Sir Pitt, saying it was unholy fun, and that she would be much more committed to reading "Thrump's Legacy" or "The Blind Washerwoman of Moorfields," "or any work of a more serious nature ; but Miss Sharp said that her dear mother often played the same game with the old Comte de Trictrac and the venerable Abbé du Cornet, and thus found an excuse for it and other worldly amusements.

But it wasn't just by playing backgammon with the baronet that the little housekeeper made herself agreeable to her boss. She has found many ways to help him. She reread, with indefatigable patience, all those legal papers with which, before coming to Queen's Crawley, he had promised to entertain her. She volunteered to copy several of his letters, and skillfully altered the spelling to suit today's usage. She was interested in everything that belonged to the estate, the farm, the park, the garden and the stables; and she was such a delightful companion that the baronet rarely took his walk after breakfast without her (and the children of course), when she gave him advice on which trees should be cut in the shrubs, the garden - them digging beds, the crops that had to be cut, the horses that had to go to the cart or the plow. By the time she spent a year at Queen's Crawley she had quite won the baronet's confidence ; and the conversation at the dinner table, which previously took place between him and Mr. Horrocks the butler, was now almost exclusively between Sir Pitt and Miss Sharp. She was almost the hostess when Mr. Crawley was away, but conducted herself in her new exalted situation with such circumspection and modesty that she did not offend the kitchen and stable authorities, among whom his demeanor was always extremely modest and affable . . She was a whole different person from the haughty, shy, dissatisfied little girl we've known before, and this change in mood showed great caution, a sincere desire to make amends, or at least great moral courage on his part. That it was the heart that dictated this new system of complacency and humility adopted by our Rebecca, it must be proven by its post-story. A system of hypocrisy, which lasts for entire years, is seldom practiced satisfactorily by a twenty-one year old; however, our readers will recall that although young in age, our heroine was old in life and experience, and we wrote in vain if they did not find out that she was a very intelligent woman.

The oldest and youngest son of Crawley's house were, like the gentleman and lady in the weather box, never at home together - they hated each other heartily: indeed, Rawdon Crawley, the dragon, had a great contempt for quite the establishment, and rarely came there except when her aunt visited her every year.

The great quality of this old lady has been mentioned. She had seventy thousand pounds and had almost adopted Rawdon. She hated her older nephew excessively and despised him like a milksop. In return, he did not hesitate to declare that his soul was irretrievably lost and was of the opinion that his brother's luck in the next world was no better. "She is an ungodly woman of the world," Mr. Crawley would say; "She lives with atheists and French people. My mind trembles when I think of her awful, awful situation, and that near the grave she should be so addicted to vanity, licentiousness, blasphemy and madness. " In fact, the old lady refused to hear her one- night lecture altogether ; and when she came to Queen's Crawley alone, he was forced to pretermine his usual devotional exercises.

" Shut up your sarmons, Pitt, when Miss Crawley comes down, " said her father ; "she wrote to say she won't stand the preaching."

"O , sir! consider the servants.

" The servants be hanged, " said Sir Pitt ; and her son thought it would happen even worse if they were deprived of the benefit of his education.

" Why , hang on, Pitt !" " Said the father to his admonition. " Wouldn't you be flat enough to let out three thousand a year from the family?"

"What is money compared to our souls, sir?" continued Mr. Crawley.

"You mean the old lady won't leave you the money?" - and who knows, but that was Mr. Crawley's intention?

Old Miss Crawley was certainly one of the outcasts. She had a cozy little house in Park Lane, and since she ate and drank way too much during the London season, she was heading to Harrowgate or Cheltenham for the summer. She was the most hospitable and jovial of old vestals, and had been a beauty in her day, she said. (All old women were once beauties, we know that very well.) She was a fine spirit, and a dreadful radical for the time. She had been to France (where Saint-Just, it is said, inspired her with an unhappy passion), and loved, forever, French novels, French cuisine and French wines. She read Voltaire and had Rousseau by heart; spoke very lightly about divorce, and more emphatically about women's rights . She had pictures of Mr. Fox in every room of the house: when this statesman was in opposition, I'm not sure she didn't throw a hand with him; and when he took office she congratulated herself on having brought Sir Pitt and his colleague from Queen's Crawley to him, although Sir Pitt had done so himself, without any problem on the part of the honest lady. It goes without saying that Sir Pitt had to change his mind after the death of the great Whig statesman.

This worthy old lady fell in love with Rawdon Crawley when a boy sent him to Cambridge (as opposed to his brother in Oxford), and, when the young man was prayed to by the authorities of the First University leaving after a two-year residency, she bought him his commission in the Life Guards Green.

A perfect and famous 'blood ', or city dandy, was this young officer. Boxing, rat hunting, five-a-side and four-man driving were all the rage of our British aristocracy at that time ; and he was a follower of all these noble sciences. And although he belonged to the household troops, who, as it was their duty to rally with the Prince Regent, had not yet shown their valor in the foreign service, Rawdon Crawley had already (speaking of play, whom he loved immoderately) fought three bloody duels, in which he gave ample proof of his contempt for death.

"And what follows after death," Mr. Crawley would observe, casting his gooseberry eyes up to the ceiling. He always thought of the soul of his brother, or of the soul of those who did not agree with him: it is a kind of comfort that is given a lot of seriousness.

Miss Crawley, foolish and romantic, far from being horrified by the courage of her favorite, always paid her debts after her duels; and didn't listen to a word that was whispered against his morals.